CHILDREN OF GOD

LUKE ROBERTS

CHILDREN OF GOD

Books may be ordered through booksellers or by contacting:
Bennett Media and Marketing
1603 Capitol Ave., Suite 310 A233
Cheyenne, WY 82001
www.thebennettmediaandmarketing.com
Phone: 1-307-202-9292

ISBN: 978-1-964296-10-4 (hardcover)
ISBN: 978-1-964296-09-8 (softcover)
ISBN: 978-1-964296-11-1 (eBook)

Printed in the United States of America

BENNETT
MEDIA & MARKETING

CHILDREN OF GOD

This book is for Robert, and Robert,
and in memory of Robert.

Two years later...

CHAPTER 1
FRIDAY NIGHT

The storm was getting closer.

A flash of lightning lit up the bedroom where Paul slept. The large boom of thunder that followed felt like it shook the house. Paul rolled over in bed and looked at the clock by his bed. 11:23. It felt like he had just closed his eyes, but he had slept for almost an hour and a half. Strong winds had hinted at the coming storm when he had gone to bed. Now the wind could be heard blowing rain against his bedroom window.

Another flash of lightning was followed almost immediately by the sound of thunder. The sights and sound of the storm reminded Paul of the old, horror movie, *Poltergeist*. He had watched it with his brothers on their basement TV decades ago. He couldn't remember how old he had been when he saw it, but he was young enough to be scared at night for weeks after watching the movie. In the movie, he remembered the storm getting closer while the little boy counted the time between the flash of lightning and the sound of thunder. When the storm was close, the toy clown attacked the little boy. After that, the old tree outside of the boy's window reached in to grab him while he screamed.

It's funny what memories stick with you from childhood, Paul thought, as he listened to the storm.

The childhood fears caused by horror films were gone. Now he loved seeing the lightning flash in the night sky, and listening to the low, rolling thunder. It was all so powerful and timeless.

The time is short.

This phrase from his dream played in his head. He had been having the same dream for the past week or two. It wasn't frightening, but he did feel restless when he woke up, and each night that feeling grew stronger. He felt as though it was time to be moving; he should be taking action, but he didn't know what to do. He wondered if the dream was about his father, but he couldn't connect a dream about Chris Rock with his father's illness.

"The time is short," he whispered in the dark, repeating the phrase that he remembered from his dream.

He gave up on the idea of deciphering the dream. Real life was hard enough right now, and he had no time to worry about a silly dream, he told himself as he lay in bed listening to the rain. He still felt tired. He closed his eyes and shifted his position in bed, trying to drift back off to sleep.

As he lay in bed, his thoughts turned to his father. He wondered if his father, whom everyone called Big Rich, was still having seizures, or if he had awakened enough to talk to the people in his room. Paul knew the nurses couldn't give him any information. He was not on the list of people who could call for updates. His brother, Richard J. Davidson Jr. (Little Rich), had made it clear to the staff that they could only give information to two people: Little Rich and his wife, Carla. He thought about calling his brother, Joe, but he didn't want to wake him, or his father, if they were sleeping.

His father had been taken to the hospital four days ago after he had a seizure at work. A CT scan of his brain had shown a mass with surrounding swelling. More tests were performed, and more specialists gave their opinions. This ultimately led to the diagnosis of a glioblastoma, a terminal brain cancer. Paul's brother, Rich Jr., was the DPOA, the designated power of attorney. He and his wife had been making the decisions about Big Rich's treatment. Paul had gone to Des Moines to visit his father after he was diagnosed with cancer. That visit had been a disaster. Paul had become more frustrated and angry each day he was there. Old wounds and angry words escalated into a physical fight between the brothers. Paul's apology to Little Rich, after their fight wasn't enough to bring peace.

His father's doctors had concluded that Big Rich did not have the capacity to make his own medical decisions. Little Rich was now legally in charge, and Paul had been banned from seeing his father.

"Father, please forgive me for being so full of anger and pride," Paul prayed in the dark. "Please open Dad's heart, and let him accept the truth about you and turn to You. I feel so bad that I failed. Father, please help this family heal, and draw us closer to You."

Paul felt better after praying, but he still couldn't fall back asleep. He could still feel the restlessness that lingered from the dream. He rolled over and looked at the clock again. 11:42.

He could hear footsteps on the floor above him. Paul slept in the basement bedroom, which had been the spare bedroom of his brother Joe's house. Joe had asked Paul to move in almost two years ago. At that time, Paul had been at the lowest point in his life. His son had been murdered, and Paul had been so consumed by despair and hopelessness that he was ready to end his own life. As Paul healed from that, he had been ready to move out of Joe's house. He wasn't going back to his old house. Instead, he found a one-bedroom apartment near the new church they had joined.

When he told his brother that he was ready to move out, Joe had teared up. That was a surprise. His brother wasn't an emotional man.

"I've been so lonely," Joe told him. Joe had lost his wife years ago in a car accident. "I don't want to date, because I still feel guilty if I do. I know that sounds crazy, but it's still there. I used to lose myself in work so I wouldn't have to admit to myself how alone I felt. But I have been lonely, and having you live here with me and the boys has brought more love and laughter into this house. We don't want you to go. I understand if you need your own place, but we want you to stay."

Life keeps getting better, Paul thought to himself. *Thank You, Father.* He quietly prayed

"Are you sure?" Paul asked. He knew his brother well enough to know that Joe wouldn't have asked him to stay if he wasn't sure about this. But the voice that made Paul doubt himself needed to hear it again.

"Please stay here," Joe said. "Life in this house is better with you here."

"You convinced me. I'm staying," Paul said, smiling at his brother.

Joe was now in Iowa, sleeping in their father's hospital room. *That's where I should be*, the guilty part of Paul's brain told him once again. He heard footsteps on the ceiling above him again. He decided to give up on the idea of getting back to sleep. He still couldn't shake the restless feeling leftover from his dream. Watching TV with his nephew sounded better than tossing and turning in bed.

He dressed and headed upstairs. He was officially in charge of his two nephews while Joe was out of town. Paul almost never told them what to do. He had been an emotional mess when he had moved in. The boys had seen him at his lowest point. They had helped comfort him when he was overwhelmed with grief. They had even brought food down to his bedroom and had encouraged him to eat. That had changed the dynamic of their relationship. It felt wrong to reprimand his nephews after they had cared for him like that.

As Paul walked into the living room he could see Joe's younger son, Luke, sitting on the couch with a bowl of salsa and a big bag of nachos. Earlier, Luke had gone bowling with friends. Paul had gone to bed before he came home. Luke was fifteen. He was very kind and compassionate. He was athletic and loved biking; he could ride for hours. Luke would always let Paul lead when they went for a ride. When Luke led, he had to keep stopping so his uncle could catch up.

Joe's other son, Jake, was two years older than Luke. Jake was a more challenging teenager to have in the house. He was surly and always seemed to be angry about something. He was a good baseball player. His team was in a spring break tournament in Arkansas. The team had left from school that afternoon. Paul didn't like to admit it, but he was glad that Jake was out of town. He had a lot on his mind, and he didn't want to deal with Jake's attitude this weekend.

Paul knew that something was wrong as he walked into the living room. Luke was watching the news at midnight. Luke had little interest in current events and rarely watched the news. Paul could see a news anchor at a desk reading the news from a teleprompter. A banner that read "BREAKING NEWS: GANG WAR IN CHICAGO. DEATH TOLL RISING" ran across the bottom of the screen. Paul walked into the room and sat down on the couch next to his nephew.

Luke looked over at him, startled.

"You scared me, Uncle Paul," he said. "I didn't hear you walking around. Did I wake you up?"

"No, I was awake," Paul told him. "What's going on?"

"My phone went off telling me about this, so I turned on the news," Luke told him. "This looks bad, Uncle Paul."

He handed Paul the remote, and Paul turned up the volume.

CHAPTER 2

SATURDAY MORNING

The TV in the office was turned to FOX News. It had been on all night. A large, bald man in a wheelchair sat behind his desk nursing a drink. The large-screen TV on the wall to his right had been repeating much of the same news throughout the night.

Chicago was burning. It was being reported that this was the result of a gang war. A push to take territory by some of the Hispanic gangs had increased the number of killings in the city last year. The death toll in the city had risen to over six hundred. The violent crime rate in Chicago didn't look any better this year. The black gangs had been losing people, territory, and money to the Hispanic gangs for over a year. The report on the news was that some of the black gangs had coordinated and pushed back hard the previous night. They had set multiple fires in areas that were considered territory of the Hispanic gangs. Many of these fires were started in apartment buildings that housed hundreds of people. When people ran from the buildings, they were shot at from the dark. When the firefighters and police came to help, they too came under fire. There were dozens of fires. After three firefighters were shot, the buildings were left to burn and the fires spread. Whole city blocks were burned to the ground. There were reports of snipers on nearby roofs shooting at police. A police helicopter had been shot down during the night. It was unclear how many police officers had been killed, but estimates put the number at over thirty. Reporters had begun keeping a safe distance from the action in the city. When the violence had first started, local news crews had rushed in to cover the story. One of them had been killed while giving a live report in front of a burning building. After that shooting, all reporting came from a safe distance and behind police lines. With each passing hour, the reported numbers of civilian and police deaths continued to rise.

The mayor's office made a ridiculous statement claiming the police were taking control of the situation and advising people to lock their doors and remain inside. Around 4:00 a.m. the Illinois National Guard had been mobilized. Armored personnel carriers, tanks, and military helicopters had entered into the city. The sound of gunfire began to die down as the sun rose over Chicago. Thousands of people, who had been fleeing the fire and the violence, now gathered in Lincoln Park. Word had gotten out that the park was safe. It was being used as a staging ground for the National Guard.

As the hours passed, and bad news from Chicago turned to even worse news from Chicago, Padre had grown quieter. He could feel his anger building. He wasn't the type of person who would have a verbal outburst. He had learned not to be hasty, but to take his time and plan a response that seemed appropriate. The plan of retaliation was never stopped by thoughts of mercy, or by doubts about whether he should leave justice to the authorities. When he was locked onto a target, he was relentless. The anger never subsided. He would have vengeance. It all became a matter of time, and the right planning

Padre looked at his phone again. He still had good contacts in Chicago. His people in Chicago were telling him that what he was seeing on TV were half-truths at best. The real situation on the ground in Chicago was much worse than what was being reported.

His drink was watered down. He was drinking whiskey, but had been intentionally diluting it as the night wore on. The only other person in his office was a beautiful, young woman with long, dark hair. She was the only one he wanted to be around right now. Lynn was smart. *No*, he corrected himself, smart was an understatement. She possessed a genius level of street smarts. She was the only person he knew who might be as tactically smart as he was. He had once utilized her talents for various jobs that he needed done right. Over time, she had increasingly assisted with planning and defining the larger picture direction of change they were trying to accomplish. Now, her help in planning an appropriate response to the Chicago attack seemed crucial. This job looked overwhelming.

"What do you think about this?" Padre asked her. He wanted her opinion before he shared his own.

Lynn sat across from him in a leather desk chair that swiveled. She hadn't said much. She knew Padre didn't want a lot of noise while he took in information and began to piece together tactical thoughts. Although the chair was pointed at the large-screen TV, she had leaned back and closed her eyes. Padre knew that she wasn't asleep;

she was concentrating, working out her own answers to questions raised overnight. She didn't open her eyes at first when she answered.

"The big questions are who and why," Lynn said. She hadn't slowed her drinking. Her words slurred as she talked. Even half-drunk, he wanted to hear her opinion. "Who is doing this? Well, it's not a group of stupid gangbangers. Those idiots will drive by in a car, spray a crowd with gunfire, and are more likely to kill an innocent kid than the person they are shooting at. Your average gang member is usually a coward who is quick to run away when shot at. These guys stood their ground when the cops came at them last night. The planning of this goes way beyond anything we have ever seen from an average gang that runs drugs and recruits kids."

She sat up and swiveled the chair to face Padre across the desk. Her eyes were now fixed on his, and her speech was less slurred as she continued.

"Whoever planned and executed this job in Chicago put a lot of time and effort into executing it flawlessly. They knew how the cops would respond to the original trouble, and they set traps that the cops walked right into. Those were skillfully laid traps. There are many well-trained, veteran cops who were ambushed and killed last night. The confirmed death toll will likely keep climbing throughout the day. I also find it interesting that they are not releasing the number of injured cops. That number will be three or four times as high as the number of those confirmed dead. I think that the National Guard was called out because a significant percentage of the police force in Chicago is currently out of commission, either dead or too injured to work.

Last night was a military-style attack on one of our major cities. I suspect those explosions were probably IEDs, and I bet that helicopter was brought down with an RPG, just like how they brought down Black Hawks back in Somalia. Whoever is behind this is using a gang war as a cover to attack this country.

Our country has a whole list of enemies that would want to do this. The list of who actually has the balls to take such action, knowing that if we identify them, we will retaliate militarily, is much shorter. My money is on the Iranians. The Russians, Chinese, and North Koreans could be behind this, but they don't think God is telling them to kill us like the Iranians. The Iranians will try to keep their hands clean, operating through a proxy of a proxy that will be difficult to trace to them, is my guess of who is behind this."

Lynn leaned back in her chair and took another drink. Even half-drunk she was still smarter than the idiots in Washington, Padre thought as he watched her. It's too bad she's not in charge of running this country. Nobody would screw with us. He smiled at the thought. Back to work, the business side of his brain reminded him. The smile disappeared as he spoke.

"Everything I've heard from my contacts confirms what you just said," Padre responded. "Now here comes the biggest question of the night." Padre paused and took another drink, finishing off his watered-down whiskey. He wasn't sure if the whiskey was making him feel warm, or if it was his growing anger.

"What do we do now?" Padre asked. The question hung in the air as he lit a cigar. He was done drinking for now. He needed some sleep and a clearer head while he planned. "I don't mean what does our country do, but what do you and I do to try to make sure another night of burning and killing like this doesn't happen again? I don't have an answer for you right now. I think we need to confirm what we know and see what action the government is taking. Let's meet back here for lunch at 15:00. I need some sleep first."

CHAPTER 3

"I'm going for a ride," Luke announced to his uncle.

Paul looked up at his nephew, expecting the question that typically followed this announcement on a Saturday morning. Usually, Luke would follow that statement by asking Paul if he wanted to go with him. They would sometimes pick a destination that involved food. Biking to Dunkin' Donuts or to a local gas station for breakfast pizza were two of their favorite Saturday morning rides. This morning Luke didn't ask if his uncle wanted to go with him. His usual calm, content demeanor was gone. He had been on edge and irritable all morning. Paul thought that the cause of Luke's irritability was the uncertainty about their spring break trip. This trip must mean more to Luke than he had thought, judging by Luke's strange behavior. Paul decided not to ask Luke about this yet; he would let Luke talk about it when he was ready.

Luke paused before opening the door to the garage. "Can we call and ask Dad about the trip now?"

"I texted your dad earlier this morning," Paul told him. He muted the TV while he talked to his nephew. News from Chicago was the only thing being talked about. "He had a long night with Grandpa Rich. He's getting some sleep this morning. He said he'll call us back when he wakes up."

"Do YOU still want to go?" Luke asked, sounding annoyed.

Paul glanced at the images of smoldering rubble on TV before answering. "Yes, I do," he answered. "I can't wait to see Nate again. He's such a good guy. He helped me out when I was hurting. I want to help him if we can."

The spring break trip had been planned for months. They were going on a trip with people from their church to volunteer at a shelter in Chicago called the Downtown Mission. They were going there to repaint the shelter, babysit children, prepare meals, and fill in wherever they were needed. Their church, and several others, were helping support the Downtown Mission. It was a Christian-based shelter that was trying to help addicts get clean and was giving homeless people a safe place to sleep. One of their youth pastors, a young man named Nate Johnson, had left their church a year ago to return home to Chicago and help out at the shelter.

A group of twelve people from their church had signed up for the trip. The plan had been to leave on Sunday morning after the 9:00 o'clock church service, arriving in Chicago in time for dinner that evening and then start working at the shelter Monday morning.

"I miss Nate," Luke said, quietly. "He helped me a lot too. I feel like I owe him so much."

Nate Johnson had sent an email earlier that morning to the members of the church who were planning on making the trip. The email read:

> Friends,
>
> We need help. We have broken windows and doors to repair and replace. There has been smoke damage to the walls and to a lot of our furniture. We need more help than ever repainting walls, moving furniture, cooking for everyone, and even taking care of wounded people. We keep trying to cram people into the shelter who need a place to stay. There are wounded people here who have been turned away from the hospital because the hospitals are full of sicker people.
>
> I think that the streets are safe now, safer even than they were before last night. The police and the army are everywhere. There are tanks and Humvees at all the major intersections. I understand if you are scared to come to Chicago right now, but I think that you will be safe in the city with this massive show of force.
>
> I'll email again early tomorrow. Hopefully it will be a quiet night. Please pray for us.
>
> God bless you,
> Nate

Paul and Luke read the email as they ate breakfast. After reading it, Luke had become more irritable as the morning wore on.

He was still standing at the door to the garage, not sure if he should say more to his uncle, or just go on his ride alone. The frustration reached a boiling point and before Luke could stop himself, he was yelling at Paul.

"This is such a load of crap!"

Paul looked at him, shocked. Luke never acted like this. Luke's brother, Jake, might behave this way, but not Luke. Paul turned off the news. Luke paused, searching for the right words.

"When my mom died, I was only ten," Luke said. "I remember all these people talking to me to try to make me feel better. I heard a lot of people telling me that she was with God, and that they didn't understand it, but that I needed to trust God. They would even quote parts of the Bible to me. These are the same people who are going to try to stop our trip to go help people who need us. THEY will want to cancel the trip, because THEY don't trust God when THEY get scared."

Luke walked into the living room and sat down across from Paul as he talked. Paul knew that Luke wasn't done. He sat quietly while his nephew continued.

"Uncle Paul, I want to go so bad that I've been having dreams about going to Chicago. And now those poor people at the shelter need our help more than ever. It makes me so mad. The people at church, who are in charge of this trip, won't even admit that they are scared and don't trust God. They are going to tell everyone how they are protecting the kids on the trip, and are only worried about the safety of the kids. I just want to tell them that the kids I know who are going aren't scared. The group text going around this morning from the high school kids going on this trip is about how we can convince all of our scared parents to still go.

A lot of the guys I know at school are going snowboarding and getting high over break. What's really screwed up is that all these scared parents would rather have us do that instead of going to help people who need us.

Luke paused again. He looked down at his shoes, slightly embarrassed, but decided to keep telling Paul what was bothering him. "This will sound weird, but I have this strong feeling that we are supposed to go to Chicago now, RIGHT NOW, not months from now. I'm worried that if we don't, then it's...it's too late."

Luke continued to stare at his shoes, shaking his head in disbelief at his own strange thoughts.

"You're right," Paul said when Luke had finished. He leaned forward in his chair. "This trip has been planned for months to help out at the shelter. You read Nate's email. Now they need our help even more, and I have the same feeling that we need to go soon. I'm not sure why, but it seems like we're racing against time to get there. I have this urge to get in the car and drive there right now. I'm still planning on going, even if the church group backs out. I've been having dreams that make me feel like I'm supposed to be there soon.

It's so strange. In this crazy dream, I'm looking up at a ten-foot-tall Chris Rock. It looks like him, but the voice is different; he sounds like Tony Evans. You're there with me. He's telling us we need to hurry, that the time is short, that we need to get to Chicago soon. I know that sounds crazy."

Luke stared at his uncle with a look of shock and confusion. He opened his mouth to speak, but didn't know where to start.

"I think you're right," Paul continued. "Most of us say we trust God, but when we get scared, we make our decisions based on our fears, not on faith. Let me talk with your dad. Go for a ride and enjoy the morning. Keep praying that God will show us what He wants us to do, and that we'll listen and have the strength to do it."

"Did you see the big, white guy, with the checkerboard head in your dream?" Luke asked quietly.

"Checkerboard head?" Paul responded, confused.

"Forget it, it's nothing," Luke said, shaking his head as he left for his ride.

CHAPTER 4

"Faster, we need to hurry! Over here, sit down."

The man talking looked to be in his late thirties, maybe early forties. He was an athletic-looking man, of average height, with flecks of gray in his well-trimmed beard. He led a man by the arm to a bench. The young man being led to the bench was small and thin, with large glasses that obscured much of his face. He looked to be in his early twenties, but could have been younger. The younger man was wearing a Mickey Mouse t-shirt that looked like it was a size too big. He was clean-shaven, had a buzz-cut, and chomped gum with his mouth open.

The two men had just made it through the annoying rituals that constituted present day security screening at a large airport. Their shoes, belts, a lap top and an iPad were in a large gray bin that had just gone through one of the scanners. The older man motioned to the bench where he wanted his companion to sit. He knelt in front of the younger man and grabbed one of the white tennis shoes from the bin.

"Give me your foot," he spoke loudly and slowly. The young man didn't move his foot. He gazed in amazement at the stores and all the people.

"Marco, PLEASE, give me your foot," the older man repeated, pointing to Marco's left foot.

The young man still didn't move. The older man finally stopped asking and grabbed his companion's left foot. He put on the left shoe and tied it. Then he picked up the right shoe. This time, the young man held up his right foot before his companion asked. The young man wore a proud smile of accomplishment as he held up his foot.

"Very good, Marco," the older man told him as he tied the shoe. He continued to speak louder and slower than his normal conversational tone. "Now we have to walk fast to get to the plane. You need to stay very close to me. Then we can get on the plane and have a snack. You can even watch Mickey Mouse; doesn't that sound nice."

They stood and Marco was led away from the security checkpoint at Leonardo da Vinci-Fiumicino International Airport. This was the busiest airport in Italy, with over thirty-eight million people passing through each year. The older, well-dressed man was nervous, but hid it well. His real name was Moshen, but he had gone by the name Antonio Russo for years. He had spent his life as a spy for his country, living most of his adult life in western Europe, primarily in Italy. He spoke fluent Italian, and his looks could pass for those of a native of southern Italy. His skills included moving untraceable money, supporting the movement of other agents, and passing on sensitive information while avoiding electronic surveillance. He had passed through this airport before. The security measures here were thorough, but Antonio had legal documentation as a registered citizen of Italy. He had a legitimate job with Chrysler-Fiat that routinely sent him traveling across Europe and to North America on business. He usually looked like any other bored, tired traveler as he made his way through the airport. He was trained to blend in, to be the person that security would overlook. He dressed in business casual attire, no better or worse than the average businessman from the area. He never carried too much cash in his wallet. He would drink a glass of wine while he waited for his flight, just like the other businessmen from southern Italy, and would eat all the food that a man from southern Italy would eat. He did not follow Islamic dietary customs while undercover.

Today felt different; today he was nervous, very nervous.

This mission was much bigger than anything he had ever been a part. The planning had been more challenging than he had expected. There were so many different pieces to arrange on this figurative chess-board. Just when he had been comfortable that the right people were in position at the right time, they had been forced to find a replacement nuclear scientist at the last minute. He had never heard of such a ridiculous request: find a last-minute replacement nuclear scientist and move him halfway around the world for the biggest attack anyone had ever planned against the United States.

The original scientist that was supposed to be on this mission had been in a car accident and was injured so badly that he had to be replaced. Antonio knew a few of the details. It had been a single car accident and the scientist was the only one in the car. Antonio had been told that the accident was caused by texting and driving. Antonio had his own suspicions that the man's conscience had played a role. Not everyone can live with the thought of killing millions of people.

The thought made him glance again at young man he led by the hand. He had been eager for the chance to go on this mission. The results of psychological tests that he had gone through disturbed Antonio, but were reassuring to his superiors, that Marco could this job. Marco was actually doing just what he had been told to do. He wasn't talking, and he kept chewing his gum and staring around looking bewildered by all the sights and smells of the airport.

Antonio wasn't surprised that Marco was remembering to play his role. The young man was smart, and Antonio knew how to leave a lasting impression with the people he trained. He smiled as he remembered Marco's training.

"You are my mentally challenged younger brother named Marco Russo," Antonio had explained to him yesterday morning at the safe house. "From now on, that is the only name that I will call you. You do not talk. This is very important to remember. YOU DO NOT TALK!" he had told the young scientist.

"Why are you yelling at me?" Hamid had asked him angrily. No one at the lab was allowed to talk to him like this. He had impressed his superiors with results at the lab. That had earned him preferential treatment. "I understand what you are saying!"

"Marco, I know that you understand me," Antonio told him. "But I am asking you to change the habits you have had your whole life. If you reflexively cry out in Farsi because you are startled or injured, you jeopardize our mission. If you even nod your head to answer someone who asks you a question in Farsi, that could get us arrested. If we are arrested, we will be tortured until we talk. We will never be able to return home again. One mistake while we are traveling could ruin everything.

I will dress you in inconspicuous clothes, and I will lead you by the hand as we travel. I will speak in Italian. It is good that you do not understand Italian. It will make your responses slower and reinforce your cover of being mentally challenged. You will chew gum with your mouth open. You will eat food with your mouth open. Do not act like you can understand anyone speaking Farsi. Do not even LOOK at anyone speaking Farsi."

As Antonio continued to yell instructions at the young scientist, the anger continued to grow inside of Marco. This man knew nothing. Marco thought. His only use was knowing a foreign language. This spy should not be speaking in this disrespectful tone. He was not the one with knowledge that could detonate the bomb. He was not the hero that made this exceptional plan work. Anger could be seen in Marco's dark eyes as Antoinio continued.

"If you make mistakes that jeopardize this mission, you will be punished. I do not want to seem cruel, but one mistake can ruin everything that we have worked so hard for. I am supposed to deliver you alive so that you can detonate that bomb. This does not mean that I will not hurt you if you fail to follow my instructions. Do you have any questions for me?" Antonio asked.

The young scientist shook his head no.

"Good. Now you are done talking until I tell you it is okay to speak. Remember, I am Antonio; you are Marco. Now, not another word, Marco."

That talk happened yesterday. Marco hadn't slept well. This morning he had woken up later than normal. It was the first morning he could remember that he hadn't been called to prayers at dawn. After using the bathroom in the small apartment, he walked into the kitchen.

"Good morning," Antonio said to him. "Would you like some coffee?" He asked in Farsi. Marco yawned and stretched.

"Yes, thank you." He answered in Farsi.

Antonio rose from the kitchen table and walked toward the coffee pot. As he passed Marco, his right hand balled up into a fist and he drove it into the younger man's stomach as hard as he could. Marco yelled out in pain as he doubled over, holding his stomach. After the punch, Antonio made him stand up straight, then drove his fist into the young man's stomach again. Marco fell to the floor holding his stomach. Antonio continued toward the coffee pot. He talked as he filled a cup for the young scientist and placed it on the kitchen table.

"You were told not to talk, but you did. You were told not to answer anyone speaking Farsi, but you answered me when I spoke Farsi. That is strike one and two, as the Americans say. I told you that I do not want to hurt you, but I need to have you very focused and following my directions. Drink your coffee. I have clothes laid out for you that you will wear today. I will finish getting ready and we will leave in twenty minutes, no later."

Antonio had not yelled at him. Marco wished he would go back to yelling instead of hitting. He looked at his watch as he straightened back up, his right hand still holding his stomach. He realized that this man would hit him again if he wasn't ready in twenty minutes. He planned on being ready five minutes early, just to be safe. He needed this man to get him to Canada, but once Marco didn't need this man's help, he was going to have his revenge for the punches in his stomach.

Marco knew how to wait for the right opportunity for revenge. It had earned him a reputation in his village. In the back of his mind, he had a vague idea of designing a low-impact explosive that would blow off Marco's lower legs, but not kill him instantly. They were both going to die, but he could make his companion die a slow, painful death. The thought of Antonio screaming in pain made him smile as he dressed.

Thoughts of revenge would have to wait. Marco was now being hurried to a plane in this massive airport. He had flown before, but he had never seen anything like the size of this airport. It seemed that exotic, new smells would entice him every few feet. He wanted to move slowly from restaurant to restaurant, trying all the delicious-smelling food. He wanted to sit at one of the tables where he could watch all the pretty young women walk by in their short skirts and low-cut tops. He had never seen so many beautiful women. He had heard stories from men he worked with at the lab about how women dressed in other countries. His head moved back and forth as he tried to watch them all as they walked by.

Antonio once again jerked Marco's arm to speed him up when he slowed down. They continued holding hands as they made their way to the proper gate. Every time Antoino pulled his arm, Marco could feel the anger he felt toward this man building.

"We need to keep moving," Antonio told him in Italian that Marco didn't understand. "Waiting in that long line made us late. When we get on the plane, you can have a snack and watch Mickey Mouse. Doesn't that sound fun?"

CHAPTER 5

SATURDAY AFTERNOON

Lynn looked at her watch again. It was 2:55 p.m. Padre had made it very clear to her early in their relationship that being punctual was important to him. It was one of the many things that had stuck with him from his military training. She knocked on the door of his office and entered when Padre yelled through the door. He had told her to come sober; he would serve drinks and a late lunch.

He had also let her know that they would be staying in. No errands to go pick people up today, no messages to deliver. Lynn knew what that meant. She didn't have to dress up. She wasn't wearing makeup. Her hair was pulled back and she had dressed for comfort.

She knew what she would see as she walked into that room. Some of the books on the shelf would change over time, but the office and the man behind that desk seemed to never change. That was fine with her. This place, this relationship, had become the most stable thing she had ever known. This was home. She felt fortunate that she had this.

"Damn, that smells good," Lynn said as she walked into the office. Padre had a big plate of ribs and potato salad in the middle of his desk, with two empty plates on either side. He had cleared the books and his computer off his desk and squeezed them onto an already overloaded bookshelf behind his desk. Most of the books were either about military history or politics. *The Death of the West* was the current book that he was reading.

Lynn pulled her chair close to the desk and started in on her ribs. Padre had made her favorite. They were brushed with honey barbecue sauce. There was a bottle of Jack Daniel's and a bottle of Jose Cuervo, with two empty glasses, sitting on the desk near the barbecue. Lynn didn't reach for the drinks. Padre would let her know when it was time to drink. She had been through this with him before. He wanted to keep a clear head when he was planning an operation. The drinks would come later.

The TV in the office was on. The big headlines of the day were being recapped. Last night's violence was being called Black Friday by the press. Reporters were still very cautious about going back into the city to broadcast. No one wanted to be shot for a story. Official briefings were being given hourly to a pool of reporters at the National Guard staging area. The throng of people who had been herded into Lincoln Park by fire and violence were too frightened to return home. Tents, cots, blankets, and food were being supplied by FEMA and the Red Cross. They had moved trailers, picnic tables, and portable toilets quickly into the park and were trying to provide people with the basics while the city violence died down and the fires were extinguished.

The president had made a statement earlier in the day about how the nation mourned the tragedy of so many lives lost in this senseless night of violence. They watched a recording of the speech as they ate lunch. The President pledged to give the state of Illinois, and the city of Chicago, all the logistical help that they needed. He talked about bringing the "lawless killers to justice." He told the nation that Homeland Security would be leading the investigation into the killings of Friday night. He had said all the right things to try to calm a nation that could still see parts of Chicago smoldering while the death toll climbed.

He ended his speech with a pledge to do whatever it took to keep the great cities of this country safe. He looked into the camera and said, "My fellow Americans, I have given the head of the Department of Homeland Security very broad powers to do whatever it takes to make the streets of Chicago safe. In Chicago, there will be a curfew, starting tonight. If it is dark, you need to be off the streets. If you are homeless, we are setting up temporary housing in areas that will be kept safe by the Illinois National Guard. All branches of the armed services will be supporting the Guard. The National Guard, and local police, will be under the command of Homeland Security."

Padre was eating slowly and watching the speech intently. Lynn seemed more interested in the ribs and potato salad than the speech on TV. She considered all these responses so predictable. The President continued.

"I will be making a trip to Chicago to visit the families of the fallen officers. These brave men and women, fighting to keep our streets safe, are heroes. To the families of these heroes, I am sorry for your loss, and we all thank you for the sacrifices your families have made. Our country grieves with you, and our thoughts and prayers go out to you. Make no mistake; your loved ones did not die in vain. We will take back the streets from the criminals and domestic terrorists who are committing violence in our great cities. We will find these criminals and we will lock them up. And we will keep them locked up.

For those who think that they can use chaos as an opportunity to commit more crimes, let me warn you that punishment will be very harsh if you commit a crime during this time - very, very harsh. We will heal this city and this great nation. We will mourn our fallen and move forward.

God bless you. God bless this great country."

Then the President had turned and walked back into the White House, ignoring a barrage of questions being yelled at him from the press. It was now time for the talking heads to give their opinion. Padre wasn't interested in this part. He muted the TV.

"What do you think?" he asked. He knew that Lynn could look like she was busy eating but would soak more of this in, and have better insight, than the idiots on TV.

"I think that he's doing all the right things to restore order," Lynn said as she wiped barbecue sauce off her fingers. She was done eating. She was full and it was time to talk. She knew that Padre would want her honest opinion about the situation before making any definite plans. She liked this part. He was one of the few people that knew she was smart and wanted to hear what she had to say.

"I think that the ACLU types will be shitting themselves and heading to court Monday morning to screw this up. I think that it is smart for him to show up in Chicago and meet with the families of the cops who were killed last night. The next election will be here soon. It will be good for his campaign if he can show that the good guys are back in control of the city. Nothing like walking around in daylight without getting shot to make people believe that the city may be a safe place to live again. People will re-elect him if he makes them feel safe."

"I agree with all of that," Padre told Lynn. "He did a better job with that speech than I thought he would. Staying with the teleprompter was a good move today. I like his instincts when it comes to dealing with a crisis. Did you see that there is going to be a response to his speech?" he asked.

"I slept in until you called me," she replied as she shook her head no. "I needed to do a little computer work, then I got ready and came here. I haven't seen any of this today. What in the world can you say in response to that speech? How can anyone disagree with restoring order in Chicago?"

Padre looked at his watch. "We will find out in about ten more minutes. The former president is going to offer his thoughts on this current crisis. Something tells me that it won't sound like what we heard earlier."

"Let me be clear," Lynn said, imitating the former president. "I was hoping that we were done with that arrogant dumbass when he left office."

"It's strange that he's speaking," Padre said slowly and thoughtfully. "I know that he's an egomaniac who loves being on camera, but we're getting close enough to the next election that the leading candidate on their side should be the one giving this response. This guy can't be going for a third term. I guess we'll find out what he has to say in a minute. Do you want a drink while we watch this?"

"Does the pope wear a funny hat?" Lynn answered.

Padre chuckled as he handed her the bottle of Cuervo.

"Let's keep it to two or three drinks until all these speeches wrap up, and we get a chance to talk about our plans," Padre instructed.

"Got it. Bottoms up," Lynn replied as she poured and downed her first drink.

CHAPTER 6

"How did it go?" Luke asked.

Luke had finished his bike ride. He had been gone longer than usual. He had mowed the yard when he came home. He had showered and was now eating a late lunch with his uncle. Paul had made them egg sandwiches with bacon and cheese, Luke's favorite. Luke knew that Paul had been on the phone with Luke's father, Joe, when Luke had gone upstairs to shower. He was eager to know if any decision about their trip to Chicago had been made. Seeing that Paul had cooked his favorite lunch made him think that bad news was coming.

"Your father's worried, but every parent would worry about their kids going somewhere that doesn't look safe," Paul told him. "One day, when you become a parent, you will realize how hard it can be to let your kids do dangerous things."

I know where this is going, Luke thought. He could feel a growing sense of disappointment.

"It doesn't help that he's had such a tough time trying to help Grandpa Rich," Paul continued. "But I told him how much both of us want to go help Nate, and I told him what Nate said about how safe the streets are right now. I asked him to trust God with this. He's been watching the news. I think that he trusts tanks and National Guard soldiers in the streets more than he trusts God to keep us safe. He finally said yes. He said you can still go!"

"No way!" Luke yelled with excitement. "That's awesome!"

Yes, it is, thought Paul as he smiled at his nephew. That restless feeling was growing. He had decided that he was going to make that trip even if everyone else in their church group backed out. He was glad that Luke was being allowed to go with him.

"We still leave tomorrow morning, right?" Luke asked.

"The plan is to meet after the 9:00 a.m. church service," Paul answered. "Whoever is going will leave from there. There was talk about renting a bus, but it's a lot cheaper if we caravan in our own cars."

Luke had finished his second egg sandwich and was now looking through the cabinets for more food. He found the nachos that he hadn't finished the previous night, and brought them back to the table.

"What were you saying earlier about seeing the checkerboard man?" Paul asked him.

Luke stopped chewing and glanced at his uncle.

"It was nothing, just a crazy dream that I only remember little parts of. Something that you said reminded me of this dream I keep having. It's weird; when I wake up, it feels peaceful, but it also makes me feel like we need to get going" Luke said as he finished the chips. "I'll start doing my laundry, then I'll pack," he told Paul.

"Are you sure you don't remember more about that dream?" Paul asked.

"I remember a super tall Chris Rock who looked real happy. I kinda remember sitting next to this huge guy who had a checkerboard tattoo on his head. He was asleep, and I could hear Chris Rock talking to you. Weird stuff. I saw a rerun of *Grown Ups 2* a few weeks ago. Maybe that's why I had the dream.

Who knows? One time I dreamed that I could fly when I was riding my bike. I don't know what that means either.

I hope we get out of church early tomorrow morning. I can't wait to get on the road. Hey, for dinner tonight let's get pizza at Mario's. We can play those old-fashioned video games that you're good at."

"Yeah, that sounds fun," Paul replied. "But we need to have the car packed and be in bed early. I don't want to be running late tomorrow morning."

"No problem," Luke answered as he walked away. "I'll get my wash done now." He stopped on the stairs and walked back into the kitchen.

"I'm so excited for this trip that I forgot about Grandpa," Luke said. "How is he?"

Paul was still sitting at the table, finishing his lunch.

"He's not doing so good," Paul said quietly. He was surprised at how quickly Luke's question brought back a wave of guilt and sadness. "After we go to Chicago, I thought we could stop by the hospital and see him on the way back. I don't think that he's gonna live very long the way he's going."

"Is that what Dad said?" Luke asked, as he sat back down at the table

"He knows that Grandpa Rich is dying," Paul answered. "Grandpa has a terminal cancer. The best that can be done is to slow it down, and I don't think he's going to get the treatment that will do even that. Your dad is getting frustrated. Your Uncle Rich is being a huge pain in the ass, worse than usual. You know how your dad likes to take charge and have everyone follow his plan. Well, he's not sleeping much because Grandpa is restless at night, and he can't get his brother to listen to him. I don't know how long he'll last up there. I wish he would give up on the idea that he can 'fix' this situation and just try to spend a few good days with Grandpa before he's gone."

"Yeah, I'd like to stop by and see Grandpa," Luke told his uncle. "I haven't seen him in a long time. I bet he's scared."

"Let's pray for him," Paul said as he folded his hands.

Luke bowed his head and folded his hands.

"Father," Paul said quietly. "Please let Dad feel Your peace, and Your love. Please open his eyes and let him see the truth, and accept Jesus as his Savior. Thank You, Father. Amen."

Paul kept his hands folded and his head bowed as he finished. He had wanted so badly to see his father become a Christian. Paul had gone to see him last week, so full of hope that he could show his father how God had changed his own life over the past two years, and explain to his father that God was ready to forgive him for all his sins as soon as he believed in Jesus. None of that had happened, and now he was losing hope that it would ever happen. He was worried that if his father died soon, he would spend eternity in hell.

Luke muttered an 'Amen' when his uncle finished praying. He continued to sit next to Paul with his hands folded.

"Uncle Paul, it looks hopeless, doesn't it?" Luke asked.

"That cancer can't be cured," Paul told him.

"That's not what I mean," Luke explained. "I mean it looks hopeless about him accepting Jesus as his Savior."

"Yeah, it's looking hopeless," Paul agreed. "He hasn't woken up enough to know where he is for days. He yells out Ira's name, even though Ira died years ago. He keeps having seizures. I don't think he knows who is in the room with him, or what they are saying."

"I hope this doesn't make you mad," Luke said slowly, "but sometimes I think God wants to make it look hopeless. That way, when God works everything out, He gets all the credit. I don't think it's as hopeless as you think, Uncle Paul. We'll keep praying for him."

With that, Luke walked upstairs to start his laundry.

I hope you're right, Paul thought as Luke walked away. He had been so full of hope that he could reach his father and watch him become a Christian just a few short days ago. That dream was dead. Paul felt defeated and angry with himself. He wiped away tears, bowed his head, and quietly prayed again for his father.

CHAPTER 7

Lynn was worried. She had never seen Padre like this. She hadn't known him when he had been in the hospital after he was shot. She had heard rumors from people who had been there during those tough days. She had heard that he had been so depressed that his friends thought he would kill himself. He had quit eating, and he didn't want to see any visitors. He would barely talk to his closest friends, and he was asking for pain medication around the clock, mainly because he wanted to be knocked out all day.

Lynn had met Padre after he had made it through that depression and was back in action. She had always known him as a fighter. It didn't matter what happened; Padre always had a plan to counterattack, and it always seemed like a good plan to her. He was a wonderful, strategic thinker who saw the world as constantly at war. He always inspired confidence, and made her think that their side, the right side, would win.

Today was different. Today he looked defeated. He kept staring down at the table, slumped over in his chair. His forehead rested in his left hand. The only time he would move was to shake his head

They had listened to the speech from the former president together. Padre had grown quieter during the speech. He had restarted the speech when it ended and handed the remote to Lynn. As they re-watched it, Padre began staring down at his desk, not saying a word, his forehead resting in his left hand. Halfway through the speech, Padre grabbed the bottle of Jack Daniel's on his desk and poured himself a large drink. Between drinks, he would occasionally glance at the screen and shake his head in disgust. When it ended, Padre asked Lynn to restart it again. That was all he said. She restarted the speech for a third time.

During the third time viewing the speech, Lynn stopped watching the TV. She was focused on Padre. She was used to him getting angry; sometimes he would even hit his desk. Today, he was just drinking quietly, staring down at his desk.

"I did not see this coming," he mumbled to himself as they re-watched the speech. "I should have, but I did not see this coming."

Lynn didn't speak. Seeing him this way bothered her more than any of the news she had seen on TV. She expected violence and chaos in the world. She had learned that this place, and this man, meant safety. He had always been so strong and confident. He was a good man, who always seemed to be trying to do the right thing. She couldn't say that about any of the men she had known before he had been in her life.

The former president had started his speech with all the expected lines about this being a day of mourning for the country. He had condemned the "attitude of despair that leads young people, without hope, into a destructive cycle of violence." He had tried to shift blame for the violence in Chicago from the criminals who had committed the crimes to the current president's policies. His wife and two daughters flanked him. After a few more minutes of predictable straw-man arguments, the president said something truly surprising.

"My wife and I have been discussing for some time how we can get more involved to try to get this nation back on the path of healing racial divisions, restoring trust in our government, and restoring hope for our young people. We have a dream of more young people heading to college and living productive lives, and fewer of them being placed in our prisons. My wife was my most trusted adviser while I was president. She is a brilliant woman, and she will be taking a more active and public role starting today, mainly because I have convinced her that her country needs her. I know that this is a painful day for her, just as it is for all Americans, but I have asked her to finish sharing our thoughts with you today."

The president stepped back, allowing his wife to step up to the microphones. He took his place on her right, with their two daughters on her left. The cameras were placed perfectly to capture this solemn family photo. As she spoke, the cameras zoomed in for a close shot of her.

"I speak to you today with a very heavy heart. I come to you as a mother, a wife, and a citizen of the beautiful city of Chicago that today lies smoldering. Parts of that wonderful city are in ruins, and there are people lying dead in the streets. I am shocked and saddened, but as I watched the footage from Chicago, another emotion began to grow: anger. Anger at policies that are leaving people in our inner cities, and in our small towns, feeling abandoned and hopeless. Anger at a system that does not protect the people who need it most. Anger at a system that works only for the rich and powerful. If you feel this anger too, I beg you, do not let it become a destructive force. Take that energy and help us build something beautiful. Help us say 'NO' to hate, 'NO' to bigotry, and 'NO' to greed.

I will be returning to my hometown of Chicago. We will mourn with the families of the victims. We will cry together and support each other as the dead are laid to rest. We will be starting an effort to help the city rebuild, and we will try to spread this movement to every city and every state in our country. We do not want to see another tragic night like the one in Chicago repeated in any other part of this nation.

I implore you again: help us build something beautiful in every corner of this country."

With that, she stepped back from the microphones, hugged her daughters, and, taking her husband's hand, walked back into their house.

Padre looked down at his desk, shook his head, and poured himself another drink.

Lynn wasn't sure what to do. She didn't want to rewatch that speech again. It seemed to bother Padre much more than she had expected, and she wasn't sure why. What she heard today was just the typical, insincere nonsense that politicians say at a time of crises. So much of it was about shaping a narrative to make themselves appear to be a compassionate savior, who would make everything better. They just needed more time, and more money. Just keep them in power and it would all be better. If it didn't get better, it was their opponents' fault, and once again, we should give them more power and much more money.

She didn't care about those speeches, she cared about Padre. She wanted to say something, but didn't know if she should. She didn't want to say the wrong thing. It was better to sit here quietly with him.

Padre finished off the drink that was in his glass. Lynn had seen him drink to relax, and often to celebrate, but this looked like a sad, cry in your beer drunk. This was the kind of drinking she saw people do when they were breaking up, or whining about something else that made life oh so horrible. She took Padre's glass and put more ice in it. Then she poured him another full drink. She put it on the table in front of him. She grabbed the Cuervo and poured a full glass for herself. She reached over and softly clinked the glasses together. She lifted her glass while she looked at Padre, but paused before taking a drink. Padre hesitated, but finally picked up the drink Lynn had poured for him. He lifted his drink up, paused, nodded at Lynn, then took a big drink of whiskey. She took a drink of her Cuervo, then they both put the drinks back down on the table. He still looked at her with his sad eyes, but Lynn knew he would come back to her and be himself again, Everybody can have a down day, she thought, even Padre. On his down day, if he didn't want to talk, then she would drink quietly with him.

On his down day, if he didn't want to talk, then she would drink quietly with him.

CHAPTER 8
SATURDAY NIGHT

Marco was dreaming. In his dream, he was back in the village where he had grown up. The people of his village lined the streets, celebrating as a flatbed truck drove slowly down the main street. The sun was bright, the day was warm, like so many days were in his village. Marco was in the back of the truck, standing up so that the crowd could see him. His brothers were in the back of the truck with him. They sat on the sides of the flatbed, cheering and chanting his name. Marco was smiling and waving at the people who lined the street. He saw old classmates, teachers, and others he had grown up with standing beneath him on the road as the truck drove slowly down the main street of his village.

He could see his father at the end of the parade route, standing above the crowd on the steps to the mosque. The mayor and the village imam were standing next to him. Even though the truck was still far from the mosque, he could hear his father clearly.

"That's my son! That's my son!" his father was proudly yelling to those around him as he pointed to Marco. The truck was now driving slowly by a row of young women. Their pretty dark eyes, which used to not notice him, now gazed at him with longing as he rode past. Suddenly he was shocked out of his dream and back to reality. His crotch was wet and cold. He was disoriented for a moment as he stared at the back of the airplane seat in front of him. A now-familiar voice spoke quietly to him in a foreign language.

"You spilled your drink on your lap," Antonio lied to him in the hushed cabin. Most of the passengers were asleep. Antonio had intentionally spilled the drink onto Marco's lap. "We can change your pants when we land. We are almost there. I brought your coloring book."

Antonio placed a coloring book depicting trucks and trains on the tray in front of Marco and gave him a box of colored markers. The mission Marco had volunteered for came rushing back to him as he looked around the plane and listened to the man next to him speaking in an unfamiliar tongue. He yawned, but did not say a word. The punch to his stomach from earlier that day remained an effective reminder not to speak.

"Here, I will color with you," Antonio said. He took a red marker and wrote on the page:

> You were speaking in your sleep in Farsi. Stay awake.
> Eat this note now.

Marco looked at the man next to him, who smiled and nodded almost imperceptibly. Marco tore out the page and put the paper in his mouth.

I hate this man, Marco thought to himself. *I will kill him. I will make him scream in pain. No one can hit him, spill cold water on his crotch, and then make him eat a page from this coloring book without paying for it.*

He had grown up being bullied by people like this man. Marco had always been small and unathletic. Once his math and chemistry abilities were discovered he was treated with respect. As he realized that he was needed at the lab, and was therefore protected, he had made small bombs to get his revenge on people that had wronged him. Most of them never saw it coming. Marco would hide the anger and resentment as well as he could, up until the moment the explosive would detonate.

This man has no idea who he is dealing with, Marco thought to himself. He reminded himself to smile at Antonio. Deception was one of the keys to revenge. It wasn't hard to smile, even while eating the coloring book. Marco was imagining Antonio, screaming in pain and dying slowly, from a low-impact explosive. The smile grew bigger.

"No, Marco," Antonio told him in Italian. "You are not supposed to eat the pages. If you can't use the markers the right way, I'll have to put them away."

Marco continued to chew the page with his mouth open. He looked away from his traveling companion, but continued to imagine ways of painfully ending his life.

CHAPTER 9

SUNDAY MORNING

Padre had spent the night in his office. He had drunk too much and then fell asleep in his chair. He was a news junkie and almost always had the TV in his office turned to one of the twenty-four-hour cable news channels. He didn't want to see any more of the news from Chicago. He was tired of watching talking heads argue about what had caused the "tragedy," and what the proper response should be. He was tired of seeing news clips of the former First Lady being replayed and reviewed very favorably by most of the commentators. He still felt defeated. Every scenario that played out in his mind came to the same depressing conclusion. The former First Lady would run for President and win the next election. The House and Senate would be controlled by her like-minded allies. He knew what the result of that election victory would be: open borders, bigger deficits, criminals not punished for their crimes, cops punished for doing their jobs, more military spending cuts, more projection of weakness worldwide, more activist judges on both the Federal bench and the Supreme Court. The way he saw it, it all meant slow death for the country he loved. The worst part for Padre was that he felt helpless to do anything about it. He wasn't used to feeling helpless. That led to feeling very depressed, and to drinking too much last night.

After Lynn had left his office the day before, Padre had switched away from the news and looked for anything distracting. He loved football, but there were no live games. He found *The Hangover* on one of the movie channels and watched it until he realized that he wasn't in the mood for a comedy. He flipped around some more until he stumbled upon *Gran Torino*. He loved Clint Eastwood when he was young, starring in westerns, or as *Dirty Harry* working the streets in San Francisco, but an older Clint Eastwood had a more thoughtful approach that he could appreciate at this point in his life. The man had an amazing screen presence at any age. Padre hadn't seen the movie in years. He poured himself one last tall glass of whiskey and leaned back into a more comfortable spot in his chair to watch the movie.

He fell asleep before the movie ended and awoke early Sunday morning with a stiff neck and a pounding headache. He hadn't planned on sleeping in his wheelchair. His doctor had been after him about pressure sores that weren't healing because he stayed in the chair too long. He had been doing a better job of caring for himself, but the previous afternoon, he had given up on everything. The TV was off. He didn't remember turning it off, but he must have hit the power button as he was falling asleep. He picked up the remote to turn the TV back on, but froze before pushing the power button. An idea that had taken root as he slept was now being evaluated by his conscious mind. He turned the idea over in his thoughts, looking for flaws from different angles.

He could fix this.

He could change the outcome of the next election and protect this country from the elected officials who were killing it from within. He had been willing to die for his country ever since he was an eighteen-year-old-kid in the Marines. Now, he was actually going to do it. He considered what would happen to his friends in the short-term and the longer term. There would certainly be a short-lived backlash from the feds. That couldn't be avoided. But his friends were tough enough to get through that. The deciding factor would ultimately be the answer to this question: What was the right thing to do for this country? He looked down at the remote in his hand. He knew what he was going to do. He was going to wipe out the politicians that would weaken his country.

"This just might work," he told his remote.

He turned back to the cable news channels with renewed energy. He didn't have much time. He needed information quickly. He began taking notes as he flipped through different news channels and surfed for more information on his computer. He created an outline of a plan and filled in some of the details that seemed solid. The President was going to speak at a memorial service for the fallen police officers. He was scheduled to arrive Monday, speak at the memorial service for the officers killed Friday night, and then fly back to Washington. The tentative time for him to speak would be at 4:00 pm Chicago time. He would be on the evening news with this address. It was good planning by his political advisers.

The former President and his wife also planned to speak at a memorial on Monday. That memorial service was now scheduled to start at noon at the downtown cathedral. They planned on having a diverse group of victims of the violence represented at the memorial. The timing of the services had been planned with the curfew in mind. Several Congressional leaders and party heavyweights would be at the memorial.

They are making this easy for me, Padre told himself. *Don't get overconfident*, he warned. *Careful planning, careful execution, one mistake could ruin everything.* This would definitely be his last mission. He would either be successful and dead, or he would fail and be in prison forever. He thought he would be sad planning his last mission, but he was excited. This would be the biggest, most important mission he had ever been a part of. The toughest part would be telling Lynn. She was the only one he would say goodbye to. She was special. He wouldn't give her any details, but she deserved a farewell. The thought made him pause in his work. He looked around the familiar room, letting memories play through his mind. He had done his part to help protect his country. His father and his fellow Marines would have been proud of him. It had been a good run. *You're a lucky man, Padre*, he told himself.

Time's up, get back to work, another part of his brain demanded. *You can rest when the job is done.* Padre wheeled himself back to a door in the corner of his office. A thumbprint recognition scanner granted him access to the adjoining room; an arsenal was locked up in here. He looked down rows of guns ranging from small handguns to M-16s. The shelves on the back wall held even more firepower. He had grenades, grenade launchers, Claymore mines, and other explosives.

In the middle of the back shelf, he found what he had been looking for. He took two boxes from the shelf and wheeled himself back to his office. He glanced at his watch. It was already 7:45 a.m.

"Alexa, look up direct flights from Kansas City to Chicago today," he told his digital assistant.

It had taken him some time to get used to using Alexa, but he now liked having "her" help him. It made working on his computer much faster. He had never been very adept on a keyboard.

"I have found fourteen flights from Kansas City to Chicago that depart today," the disembodied voice told him.

He wheeled himself to one of the chairs that sat in front of his desk and transferred himself into it. He opened the boxes, turned over his wheelchair, and began making special modifications to it. He glanced at his watch again as he worked. The morning was going by too fast, and there was so much to do.

CHAPTER 10

The right side of the Greyhound bus was covered with a thin film of dust. It had been traveling through the night from Denver to Kansas City. A warm, south wind had been rocking the bus as it rolled east down I-70. The wind carried dust from Oklahoma and Kansas farm fields, coating the side of the bus. The bus had turned off the interstate and was slowly winding its way through the downtown streets of Kansas City. The low, steady hum of the engine had been replaced by the sound of squealing brakes and the feel of slow wide turns.

The driver glanced again in the rearview mirror at the two men seated in the rear. He had been keeping a close eye on them. He had been driving this route for years. After the new prison had opened in Hays, he had seen men like them too often on his route. They had tell-tale prison tattoos he had noticed when they boarded. He had warned the other passengers to move closer to the front of the bus before the stop at Hays. He had seen these released prisoners board and stir up trouble. He now carried a gun under his seat. He knew he could be fired if the company found out about the gun, but he wanted to be prepared if one of these criminals caused trouble when no help was around in the middle of Kansas.

In the mirror, he could see that the big white guy with the strange tattoo was stirring. He had taken a seat on the left side of the bus. The skinny black man, who bore a striking resemblance to Chris Rock, sat across the aisle from him. They had taken seats several rows behind the other passengers. The black man had not slept, but he had kept to himself. He looked eager to disembark the bus. He was leaning forward, looking like he was ready to stand up before the bus came to a stop. The white guy yawned and started talking to him. The smaller man leaned back in his seat. The driver strained to hear what they were saying, but the white guy was speaking quietly. The driver shot another glance in their direction to make sure they weren't bothering the other passengers, then focused his attention back on the road as he made the final turns to the bus terminal.

When the bus stopped, the other passengers stood and grabbed their bags. The white man in the back yawned again and rolled his neck from left to right as he looked around.

"JD, check it out," he pointed out his window at a taco truck. His voice was low and raspy. "Breakfast burritos - it's our lucky day."

"Sam, I don't get you," JD answered. "How can you be thinking about food? There's so much going on. I still can't believe this is happening. I couldn't sleep. I kept asking God to help me say and do the right thing today. I was thinking about some of the witnessing I've done with other prisoners. I was going over what I thought I did right and what I could have said better. I can't believe it's all playing out like you said it would. This is overwhelming stuff man, overwhelming. I've got all this running through my head all night. I can't sleep, and all you can think about is eating food from a truck?"

"Brother, you worry too much," Sam answered. "Let's pray, then we can grab some food and get moving. We have a lot of ground to cover today."

Sam folded his hands and bowed his head. JD did the same in the seat next to him.

"Father, thank You for this day," Sam prayed. "Thank You for opening our eyes when we were blind. Thank You for using us to spread Your word and to glorify You. Please keep us strong and help us to obey You. Please guide us on this journey. Amen."

They unfolded their hands and stood up. The other passengers had already left the bus. Sam stood and patted his friend on the shoulder.

"You'll do fine," he said as they walked off the bus. "Now, let's get some burritos. I'm starving."

CHAPTER 11

Marco awoke in a strange, dark room with a full bladder, slightly disoriented. He looked around the ship's cabin. He didn't know the local time, but it was daylight outside. He could see lines of light around the edge of the heavy curtains as the boat rocked gently. Marco had been told not to touch the curtains. No one was to see him until they were far away from land. He stood and looked through the gap that the curtain didn't cover. He could see other boats docked near their boat. As he made his way to the bathroom, he realized that the slight rocking motion intensified his nauseated feeling. He hadn't noticed that feeling when he first woke up.

He had no idea how long he had been asleep. He remembered landing and collecting their bags. He had been exhausted. Antonio had been speaking Italian, which Marco didn't understand. He had remembered to act the part of the mentally challenged brother who couldn't speak. It was getting easier. Marco had been so tired that he felt like he could fall asleep standing in line at customs. He hadn't understood anything that had been being said in Italian, French, or English. *What is wrong with these people?* his sleep-deprived brain had asked himself. They keep speaking louder and slower, thinking I will understand a different language if they just yell it loud enough at me. For some reason, that thought had made him laugh out loud. Every time the strange people in the airport had talked to him in that crazy-loud-nonsense language, it had made him laugh again.

The sleep deprivation is working well, Antonio thought as he watched the young man. If he didn't know better, he would have guessed that the young man really was mentally challenged.

Antonio had led him by the hand through the airport to baggage claim. Once they had their bags and were outside, Antonio lit a cigarette. Marco looked at it longingly as his traveling companion inhaled deeply. Antonio's eyes warned him that it was still not safe to speak freely. He shook his head ever so slightly to tell Marco not to ask for a cigarette. Marco was exhausted and tired of this man telling him what he could and couldn't do. He started reaching for the pack of cigarettes that Antonio held.

Antonio felt a flash of anger as Marco reached for the cigarettes. Letting his companion smoke would blow the cover of being his mentally challenged little brother. Antonio realized that physical violence was also out of the question as they stood in front of the airport waiting for a car. Several other people were out on the sidewalk with them, waiting for rides. Any violence would be noticed, and the police might be notified. The mission could end here if Antonio wasn't careful. He held the pack of cigarettes higher and away from Marco. He made a tight fist, crushing the pack of cigarettes in his hand. He smiled at the disappointed look on Marco's face.

I look forward to hurting you, Marco thought, as he glared at his traveling companion.

Marco was no longer thinking about having a cigarette. He felt more nauseated as he emptied his bladder in the tiny, rocking bathroom on the ship. He was eight time zones away from home, and he wasn't sure if it was time to eat. *Maybe some food would make me feel better*, he thought. He didn't see any food on the small table in his cabin. He was too tired to look further and crawled back into bed. Antonio was sleeping in the bottom bunk. Marco stepped onto a wooden crate to get back into the top bunk. The crate was one and a half feet high, three feet wide, and two feet deep. When they first arrived, Marco stood on the crate to reach the top bunk. Antonio had yelled at him and pulled him off the crate, worried that Marco would damage or detonate the nuclear bomb inside the crate. Marco knew that the bomb was incredibly powerful, but also stable until detonated. Antonio, who had never seen a nuclear bomb, had been much more worried that the bomb would detonate if it were mishandled. Marco enjoyed seeing the fear in his companion. He stood back on the crate and jumped on the crate, as high as the low ceiling on the ship allowed him to jump. When Marco landed on the crate, Antonio fell backward onto the lower bunk, cringing in fear and irrationally holding up his arms to protect himself. Marco jumped two more times onto the top of the crate, laughing at the cringing spy. Then he had climbed into the top bunk and had quickly fallen asleep.

This time, when Marco climbed back up to the top bunk, he had trouble falling asleep. Every little rock of the boat made his nausea worse. He jumped down from the bed and ran back into the bathroom. He emptied the little food that was in his stomach into the toilet. When he finished, he lay back down on the top bunk, feeling much better. He must have eaten something at the airport that was making him sick, he thought, as he fell back asleep.

CHAPTER 12

It had been a very disappointing morning. Paul was beginning to doubt that he was doing the right thing. If everyone else who was supposed to go on this trip thought it was too dangerous, maybe they were right; maybe he was wrong. Paul and Luke had gotten the car packed for their trip and were at the early church service. None of the people who had agreed to go to Chicago with them were at the service. The plan had been to go to the early church service, pray, eat breakfast, and caravan together to Chicago. Instead, a group text full of excuses for not going on the trip was circulating. Nearly every text had the same theme:

> We want to help, but it seems too dangerous. We want to be responsible and protect the children on this trip. We will definitely go help at the shelter when it is safe.

After the service, Paul and Luke had waited at the back of the church where they had originally planned to meet with everyone who was going. They waited impatiently for fifteen minutes. No one joined them. They left alone. It was a relief for Paul to finally leave the church. He somehow felt that they were going to be late if they didn't leave soon

"I'm proud of you, Uncle Paul," Luke told him. "I thought you would change your mind this morning when everyone else chickened out. I'm glad you're doing the right thing."

"I'm not 100% sure that this is the right thing. It feels like it is, but everyone else disagrees. If it doesn't look safe when we get there, we are going back home. There is no way I want to be responsible for anything happening to you."

"Thanks Uncle Paul," Luke replied. "But maybe it's the right thing to do, even if it doesn't look safe. Let's keep trusting God."

Paul shook his head without saying a word and kept driving.

They had already filled the gas tank before church. They had planned on eating breakfast with the group that was going to Chicago. The plan had changed to grabbing a breakfast sandwich at a drive-through and getting on the road. Paul finished his breakfast in a few oversized bites. While he was still chewing, he reached for his large Diet Coke to wash it down.

"I'm having this crazy déjà vu feeling," Luke said as he watched his uncle reach for the drink.

Paul looked over at his nephew when he heard this. He had been lifting the Diet Coke by the lid. The lid came off, and it dumped onto his lap. Paul swore as he looked down and tried to sweep the ice and Diet Coke off his seat and onto the floor.

"Look out!" Luke yelled.

Paul had been looking down at the spill. When his nephew yelled, Paul looked up to see three deer start to run across the road, right in front of the car. Paul swerved to the right to avoid the deer and hit the brakes. The car started sliding on the gravel shoulder. The shoulder sloped away from the road into a grassy ditch. Paul watched as the car kept sliding downhill, moving from the shoulder to the grassy ditch. In his mind, it felt like it was happening in slow motion. He was worried that the car would start to roll when the wheels hit the soft dirt near the gravel shoulder. In his peripheral vision, Paul could see that the deer had stopped on the other side of the road and were watching the car slide out of control. He took his foot off the brake, trying to regain control of the steering. He turned the wheel to the left, trying to get back on the road. It didn't work. The momentum of the car continued the slide toward the grass. The car jolted to a stop as the right front fender hit a rock.

Paul put the car in park and turned off the engine. He looked over at his nephew, his heart still racing. "Are you okay?" he asked.

"Yeah," Luke answered. "Are you?"

Paul nodded yes. "That was scary," he told his nephew.

Paul unbuckled and opened the door. His phone had fallen on the floor and was submerged in a puddle of Diet Coke.

"Damn it," Paul muttered as he picked up the phone. The phone refused to turn on when he pushed the power button. "I think I just ruined my phone."

He put the phone in the empty drink holder. He used the cup to scoop out Diet Coke and chunks of ice from the floor.

"Let's see how bad this is," he said as he exited the car.

They walked around the car. The front right fender had come to rest against a large rock. The rock had pushed the fender into the front tire.

"Maybe we aren't going to Chicago today," Paul said as he evaluated the damage to the car. "We need to call a tow truck. I can't even drive this to a garage without ruining that tire."

I'm having this crazy déjà vu feeling, Luke had said right before the accident. The words came back to Paul as he looked at the car resting against the rock. He could feel it too. It felt like he had seen this before. The strange memory fragment felt peaceful, even though he had just been scared and sliding out of control.

"Uncle Paul, look."

Paul looked to where Luke was pointing. They had been driving up an incline when the accident occurred. Over the top of the hill, Paul could see a head bobbing up and down. He and Luke watched as the figure came closer. It was a man who looked very much like Chris Rock. As he came closer to the top of the hill, they could see that he was riding on the shoulders of another man. The man on the bottom was a very large, white man with a strange tattoo covering the top of his bald head.

"Checkerboard man," Luke whispered.

The man who looked like Chris Rock had a big smile on his face. He was wearing dark blue sweat pants and a hoodie that matched. He was pointing at Paul and Luke and talking in an excited voice to the man beneath him.

"No way!" he yelled. "No freakin' way! I can't really believe what I'm seeing. You were right, Sam. You told me, brother. You told me, and I said I believed you, but I didn't 100% believe you. This is amazing!"

The big man finished jogging up to Paul and Luke. His face was red, and he was struggling to breathe. He fell to his knees when he stopped. The man who had been riding on his shoulders stepped off and walked up to Paul and Luke with his hand outstretched. He limped every time he put weight on his right hip.

"My name is JD," he said, shaking their hands. "And this is Sam," he nodded at the larger man standing behind him.

Sam turned toward the grass and began throwing up.

"I warned you about those breakfast burritos," JD said over his shoulder to his companion. "I told you that six was too many when we had all that walking to do. And how can you trust food from a truck?"

Sam wiped his mouth with the back of his sleeve and shot an angry look at his friend.

"Yeah, that's right. You should get angry with me 'cuz I'm the one who MADE you eat too many greasy breakfast burritos this morning. No, wait a minute, I'm the one who told you to slow down and not eat so many!"

Paul and Luke were stunned. Luke was staring with his mouth agape.

"You look a lot like your dad," JD told Luke as he stood in front of him, holding his shoulders. "I have heard so many good things about you." As he said this, he gave Luke a big hug. Luke did not hug back. He looked at his uncle, wondering what to do. Paul shrugged as he watched the stranger hug his nephew.

"I'm sorry," JD said, letting go of the boy and limping back a few steps. "I don't want to scare you, but I'm so excited. I have heard even more about you," JD said, turning his attention back to Paul. "Joe is so blessed to have a brother like you. He told me how God is working in you, turning you into a man of deep faith, and how that has helped grow his faith. He told me about the day you two were baptized. Brother, I cried when he told me about that wonderful day."

"I'm sorry, who are you?" Paul asked.

This question caused JD to laugh. The sound surprised Paul. It was a big, deep, fat-man laugh that came out of the body of this skinny man limping in front of him.

"Where are my manners? I am JD White," he said, bowing at the waist. "Lenora White was my mom. Your brother took care of her a few years ago when she was dying from cancer. After she passed, your brother drove out to the prison in Hays and hand-delivered a letter to me from my mom. Man, that letter was the most beautiful thing I ever read. It came at just the right time in my life."

"I remember Joe telling me about your mother. She sounds like a special lady," Paul said.

This caused JD to laugh again.

"She was a drunk and a lousy mom for most of her life," JD said surprising Paul. "She had a lot of painful things to deal with in life, and when she was younger, she drank to numb that pain. But she found Jesus later in life and became a child of God, a lot like I did. I'm so glad God opened her eyes. I'm so glad I get to see her again in heaven. I wasn't a very good son. I think I have a lot to apologize for when I see her.

She wrote me this beautiful letter telling me how sorry she was for all the mistakes she'd made, and she told me how much she loved me. She wrote about finding forgiveness for all her sins, and being ready to see Jesus when she died. She urged me to ask for forgiveness and to believe that Jesus died for me. She wrote about praying hard that I would become a child of God. She told me that she couldn't wait to see me and hug me again one day."

JD was tearing up as he spoke.

"She didn't know that God had been working on me, mainly through my brother Sam. I was a new believer at the time she wrote to me, and her letter helped me a lot. I'd been up at night praying for her, and then I find out that she's been praying for me. All that I was learning about a loving God who had a plan, and was working all things for good in the life of his believers, it's like that letter was the proof of all of that. I wrote your brother a long thank you note for delivering that letter to me in Hays, and I told him that I had become a believer. I even got baptized."

"I saw you," Luke broke in. He was staring at Sam. The man was massive. He was 6'4" and weighed almost 340 lbs. He wore a baggy white t-shirt, but the large muscles on his back, chest, and shoulders could be seen under the shirt as he moved. Sam nodded his head yes and crossed his arms. Tattoos covered the visible skin on his head, neck, arms, and hands. The large tattoo that covered the top of his head looked like an irregular checkerboard. There was a long scar across the front of his neck that looked like it should have been a fatal wound.

"Sam's not much of a talker," JD said, answering for his friend. "He had an injury to his voice box years ago. But he was the one who told me that we would meet you two today. He sees things. He says that God shows him stuff in his dreams. He told me that you were going to Chicago to help after the Friday night violence, and that you would give us a ride. He also told me that we need to get there fast if we're going to help. The strangest part is, he told me this two weeks ago. TWO WEEKS AGO!" JD paused to let the news sink in before continuing. "Do you remember what you were thinking about two weeks ago? Well, it wasn't Black Friday, 'cuz two weeks ago, nobody thought that Black Friday was gonna happen."

As Paul realized what JD was telling him, his gaze shifted to Sam. He couldn't believe that this mountain of a man could see the future. He must have known the people who had planned the violence in Chicago, Paul thought as he digested the information. But when he looked at these two men, he was somehow sure that he could trust them. He still couldn't shake the feeling that he had seen this before. The deer, the spilled drink, and the skinny Chris Rock look-alike with the deep voice all seemed very familiar.

"We actually were going to Chicago, but we were in a little wreck," Luke told them. "Uncle Paul thinks we need a tow truck to get our car to a garage."

Sam walked around the car, examining the damage. He nodded and gave JD a thumbs up sign after he had circled the car.

"Does the engine still run okay?" JD asked Paul. "Is the only problem that fender?"

"I think so," Paul answered.

"Well, we need to get moving," JD told him. "If we can get your car running right now, will you give us a ride?" JD asked. "The time is short, brother. We've gotta go."

That was the phrase, Paul thought, as he stared at JD. That was the phrase he remembered from his dream. He realized that it was JD's voice that he'd heard in those dreams. *How can that be*? he asked himself as he stared at JD in amazement.

Paul looked from JD to Sam. His eyes stayed on the huge man with the strange tattoos and the neck scar. The man was standing with his arms crossed. On both of his forearms, Paul could see tattoos that read "LUKE 23:43." The big man smiled at him and nodded his head.

I hope this is the right thing to do, Paul thought. He could feel the urge to get to Chicago growing stronger. He hoped that wasn't clouding his judgment.

"You've got a deal," Paul told them. "If you can get this car on the road, we will give you a ride.

CHAPTER 13

SUNDAY AFTERNOON

I think I'm dying, Marco thought as he lay on his bunk. He stopped fighting the urge to throw up. He rolled over and emptied a small amount of green bile into a bucket that had been left by his bed. He had to concentrate not to fall over sideways as he threw up. When he finished, he wiped his mouth with the sleeve of the oversized Mickey Mouse T-shirt that he was still wearing. This new discolored area on the sleeve added to other vomit stains on the shirt.

"I'm impressed."

Antonio's voice floated over from the nearby table. He didn't want to turn his head and look at the man. Turning his head made the nausea and vertigo worse. Also, he had developed a loathing for his traveling companion. Somehow, he blamed Antonio for his misery.

"I have seen people who have been seasick before, but I have never seen anyone as miserable as you. How many times have you thrown up today – ten, twelve? Whatever the number, it has gone from entertaining to annoying. Who knows, maybe you have a case of food poisoning, and it's not just seasickness. Although, we ate much of the same food and I'm not sick."

Antonio paused, then smiled as he continued, "Now that I think about it," he said, "you did eat that page from the coloring book, and you didn't share that with me. Perhaps that is why you are so sick."

Antonio laughed to himself as he teased the sick young man. He was sitting at a table playing solitaire with a worn deck of cards.

"By the way, you can speak freely now in Farsi," he said as he laid down another card. "The two-man crew is up on deck. There is no cellular coverage here, just the shortwave radio in this room, so they can't call and tell anyone about our conversation, which these Canadians will not understand anyway."

There was silence for a few moments, then Marco said quietly, "I need medicine. I can't do my job when I feel this sick and weak. I'm too dizzy to stand up."

"I have good news and bad news for you," Antonio said as he finished winning the game. "I like that phrase. It fits well with so much of the news that I tell people." He shuffled the cards as he talked.

"I brought medical supplies that can help you. I have IV fluids to hydrate you, medicine to help with your nausea, and even a medicine that will help with your dizziness. That is the good news. The bad news is that I could only bring a small amount of these medicines. If they are used now, and you get sick again tomorrow, I will not have more medicine to give you when you need to detonate the bomb. So, you will have to endure one more miserable night. Don't worry.

Tomorrow you will feel better and be able to function, when we are close to Chicago."

Antonio shuffled the cards to begin another game. His hands handled the cards, but his eyes stayed on the young man in the top bunk. He wasn't sure if Marco believed his lie. Antonio had a good supply of medicine. He could give them to him now and have plenty to use tomorrow, but he didn't like this man, and he definitely didn't trust him. Having him sick and incapacitated on the top bunk allowed Antonio to rest a little easier. The psychological tests on Marco had been disturbing, but a disturbed young psychopath was probably the ideal candidate when the goal was to kill millions of innocent people, Antonio thought as he dealt the cards. He had been able to watch some of the tests that Marco had to pass before he was allowed to participate in this "glorious mission". One of the last tests was designed to evaluate his loyalty to the faith. The man running this test told Marco that a young woman, about Marco's age, had betrayed the faith. She had been raised in a good Muslim family, but she had been found proselytizing (she had given a Bible to her friends) and working with the Americans. His job was to kill her. They gave him a nine-millimeter pistol with one round. They had taken off the safety, handed him the gun, and told him to go into her cell to give her what her crime deserved. He had been given no other instructions.

She was sitting in a chair with her hands cuffed behind her. Marco walked in and, without speaking to her, put the gun against her stomach. She began crying, begging him to stop. He paused with the gun against her stomach, listening to her cries for mercy. Antonio was watching the test with a small group in the next room. Antonio thought that Marco would say something to her, or maybe realize that he couldn't kill this young, helpless girl. Without warning, he pulled the trigger. The shot knocked her onto the floor on her side. She lay crying out in pain as blood spread around her. He left her cell without saying a word.

The people running this test had questioned him about the shot. Knowing he had only one bullet, why shoot her in the stomach instead of the head or chest? Marco explained that she deserved to die as slowly and painfully as possible for betraying the faith. He had passed the test, and now this cruel little man was here to detonate a nuclear weapon and annihilate a major American city. The man seemed small and helpless to Antonio, but he reminded himself never to take his eyes off this sadistic killer.

"There is a storm coming this evening, and the waves should calm down after that. Maybe that will help you feel better, even before you get the medicine," Antonio said as he started his new game.

"I hate the water," Marco mumbled. He was lying on his side, holding his stomach, facing the wall. "I want to be back on land."

"I love the water," Antonio told him. He looked up from his game as he talked to Marco's back. "Some of the best days of my life happened on yachts in the Mediterranean. Some of my rich friends would take us out to play on their boats. We would eat and drink and swim in the warm water. We would make love to beautiful women in the afternoon, then we would eat a gourmet dinner and drink wine as the sun set over the water. These waves bring back the taste of the food, and the touch of the women. Those were good days."

Marco managed to roll over in bed and face Antonio. The act of turning brought back dizziness and nausea, but he pushed through the symptoms. Anger flashed in his dark eyes as he glared at Antonio.

"How can the Imams pick a man such as you to be used for a mission like this? You are no better than an infidel! No, you are worse! You know the truth and yet you live the life of an infidel!"

"Maybe you are right," Antonio answered quietly, but his voice rose as he continued. "Maybe I do need a moral lesson from an angry, frustrated little virgin who makes bombs. You hide in your little lab like a mouse and give us real fighters bombs so we can do the dirty work. You never get your hands dirty, you never face the men who can shoot back at you. You never see your friends get taken by the police to be tortured in prison! I have done that work. I live the life of an infidel because I am supposed to blend in and look like one of them. I did enjoy some of those days of pleasure. Does that mean that you are better than me? No! If you had the chance to live my life, you would have enjoyed the same wine and the same women. Now it is time for you to shut your mouth. If I catch you looking at me like that again, I will slap you."

Antonio rose and walked out of the cabin, slamming the door as he left.

CHAPTER 14

Cornfield after cornfield continued to pass by at 80 miles an hour. Luke had been in the back seat of his uncle's car for hours. They had traveled from Missouri to Iowa, and would end the day in Illinois.

The trip had taken a strange twist. He was sitting next to Sam, a massive man who had just been released from prison, with strange tattoos on his head, neck, and arms. The man had fallen asleep shortly after the trip had started. He had stayed awake long enough to tell Paul to go faster.

"Keep it moving," Sam had told Paul. "We need to get there before dark."

Sam watched as Paul increased the car's speed. After he was satisfied that Paul was going fast enough, he flashed Paul a thumbs-up sign, then crossed his arms, leaned his head back, and fell asleep. He had started snoring two hundred miles ago. The snoring would occasionally pause when the car changed lanes.

Paul was driving with JD in the passenger seat next to him. JD wasn't sleeping; in fact, he had been talking almost nonstop since the trip started.

"I've never seen so much corn," JD told Paul. "I've never been to Iowa before. The only two states I've ever been in are Kansas and Missouri. For the past twenty years, I've been stuck in the middle of Kansas in prison. Man, it feels good to be on the outside. I used to dream about this day. My dreams were nothing like this. I was going to go back to my old neighborhood and get together with some old friends to party. I planned to get high as a kite for days. I was going to eat some good home cooking and drink with my friends. Man, I had a whole list of stupid things I couldn't wait to do. I was going to look up some girls I used to know and party with them. If somebody told me I'd be in a car with three white boys in the middle of Iowa, I woulda laughed my ass off.

Man, I used to hate white people," JD continued, shaking his head. "It was so stupid. I remember fighting with other gangs, mostly other young black kids like me, and even killing each other over nothing. But everyone around me hated white people, so I did too. Once I found God, I saw how ignorant I'd been. I used to be so ashamed of who I was. Sam helped teach me about a God of forgiveness and love and second chances. I remember, one day I was sweeping up in the infirmary, and I'm listening to Tony Evans teach on Luke 15. That's the Prodigal Son story. I listened to him open up all this rich meaning in the story that I never understood before. Next thing I know, I'm standing there crying, crying so hard I'm shaking. And Sam comes over and puts his big arm around me. He doesn't say anything. He just stands there while I cry. When I'm done, he pats me on my back and says to me, "Amen, brother. Amen." Then he walks away and goes back to work. When he started looking out for me, the guys in prison thought we were queers. If they ever said anything, Sam would just smile at them and walk away. I guess he thought it was funny that they called him gay after all the stuff he did before he went to prison. That boy was seriously horny and loved the ladies when he was young."

JD paused and glanced back at his friend. They were changing lanes again, and Sam had stopped snoring. Sam raised his head and looked around the car.

"How long until we get there?" he asked.

"About four hours if we keep going this fast," Paul answered.

Sam nodded his head. "Good. That will get us there on time"

On time for what? Paul wondered. *What happens if we get there late?* He wanted to be careful and not offend these men. He realized that they were far from help, his cell phone wasn't working, and these men had just gotten out of prison. Giving them a ride had seemed like a good idea this morning, but the sight of Sam in the rearview mirror was making him second-guess that decision. He decided that he would carefully ask about why they were in such a hurry to get to Chicago.

"Damn, Sam!" JD spoke up before Paul could ask his question. "Your puke breath is killing me! You are stinking up this whole car every time you open your mouth. We need to stop and get some gum. I'll buy. And I could use a bathroom break too."

"Yeah, and we could use some gas," Paul said. "The last sign said food and gas at the next exit. Let's pull off there."

"Is your car driving, okay?' Sam asked.

"It's running great," Paul answered. "I've never seen anyone pull a fender out with his bare hands like that."

Sam simply shrugged his big shoulders in response.

Luke had an earbud in his left ear. He had been listening to music when Sam woke up. He scrolled for other music after the song ended. Sam watched as he picked a song and began to play it.

"Is that an iPhone?" Sam asked, covering his mouth.

"Yeah. It's an older one, but it still works okay," Luke told him.

"I've never seen one before," Sam told him. "I've seen the ads, and I've seen people use them on TV, but I've never seen one in person. The guards weren't allowed to have them at work."

Luke unplugged the earphones and held the phone up so that Sam could see.

"Here's how you use it," Luke said, showing him how to search on Safari. He then showed him how to ask Siri a question. He even took a short video of the passing cornfields and then filmed everyone in the car. When he was done, he played it back for Sam.

"That is amazing," Sam said as he watched Luke navigate the iPhone. He was still covering his mouth because of his bad breath.

"It sounds better with the earbuds in," Luke told him. "Do you want to put them in and listen to it?"

"Me? Really?" Sam asked, surprised at the offer.

"Of course," Luke answered. "What kind of music do you like?"

Sam was grinning with excitement as Luke gave him the earbuds.

"We don't get a chance to listen to a lot of music," Sam told him as he put the earbuds in. "I like Christian music and country, but I'll listen to anything."

Luke scrolled on his phone. Sam was still grinning with excitement.

"Here's something I think you'll like," Luke said as the music started.

Sam closed his eyes and nodded his head to the music as Toby Mac sang "I was made to love you". When the song finished, Sam took the earbuds out. He blinked back a few tears as he looked out the window. It had been a long time since someone had been kind to him. The other inmates would do something for him out of fear, or if they wanted something in return, but nobody in his world did anything just to be nice. He knew that his looks frightened people, and yet this high school boy was sharing his iPhone with him, and didn't want anything in return. Sam hadn't expected this kindness, and he hadn't expected it to affect him this way. *Maybe it's because I know how this trip ends,* he thought to himself, *maybe that is why I'm so emotional.* He knew what he wanted to hear next; it was a song that always brought him comfort.

"Thank you," Sam told Luke when he trusted himself to speak again. "Can I listen to one more song?"

"Sure," Luke answered. "Do you know what song you want?"

"It's called *No Longer Slaves,* the Zach Williams version," Sam answered. "Do you know that one?"

"Yes, I do," Luke told him, as he brought it up on his phone. "I like that one too. Got it. Put those earbuds back in."

"This is my favorite," he told Luke as he placed the earbuds back in his ears. As the music started, he closed his eyes.

"This is one of my favorites too," JD told Paul in the front seat. "Even Sam's awful singing can't ruin this song."

He joined in, singing along with Sam. "You unravel me, with a melody. You surround me with a song of deliverance, from my enemies, 'Till all my fears have calmed. I'm no longer a slave to fear, I am a child of God. I'm no longer a slave to fear I am a child of God."

When the song finished, Sam handed the earbuds back to Luke. He wiped away tears and wiped his running nose with the back of his hand.

"You okay?" JD asked him from the front seat.

Sam was quiet for a moment as he blinked back more tears.

"I'm okay," he answered. "It's just hard to believe this is all really happening. I'm still stunned that God would give us this chance."

The car slowed and eased onto an off ramp. Just off the interstate, a McDonald's, a gas station, and a Subway could be seen. They were clustered together, sharing one large parking lot.

"Thank you, that was good, real good. I love that song," Sam told Luke. "It has helped me on some rough days." He turned his attention to Paul and JD. The tears were gone. He was back to business. "Luke and I will get the food. You two get the gas and get us ready to leave. We need to leave before the police come. They will slow us down, and we don't have much time. It's important that we keep moving."

Paul didn't see any police officers as he pulled up to a pump, but he didn't want to argue with a massive, possibly paranoid man who had just gotten out of prison. He gave Luke his order for food and started pumping gas. By the time he had filled up and gone to the bathroom, Luke and Sam were back.

"Let me at that food!" JD yelled at Sam and Luke as they approached the car with drinks and a bag of fast food. "I am sooo hungry!"

Sam was holding the food. Luke had a drink holder with four drinks. Sam shook his head no.

"We need to get on the road, then we eat," Sam said as he opened the door and climbed back into the same spot in the back seat.

Paul started the car and left the gas station. As he turned onto the on-ramp, he could see two highway patrol cruisers getting off the interstate, heading for the gas station they had just left. He glanced at Sam in the rearview mirror. Sam winked at him in the mirror.

"Good job, Doc," he told Paul, as he opened the bag and started handing out food. "Now let's get the speed back up. We don't have to worry about cops again until we get close to Chicago."

Paul took the speed back up to 80 and set the cruise control. Sam nodded his approval as the speed increased, then finished handing out the food.

"Do you mind if I pray?" Sam asked them.

They had all been opening their food. They paused and bowed their heads.

"Father, thank You for this food. Thank You for new friends and for the chance to go to Chicago to do Your work. Please give us the strength to obey You, and to bring glory to You. Amen."

"Amen, brother," JD repeated.

They were quiet as they ate. After finishing his sandwich, JD held his fries up to his face and inhaled deeply.

"Man, I love that smell," JD told them. "This reminds me of being a kid. I remember being thirteen, maybe fourteen years old. I'd get high with my friends and we'd walk a few blocks to this McDonald's in the neighborhood. We would get free fries from my friend's sister who worked there. We would act like fools and try to show off for the girls. It's funny how a smell can bring back all those memories. I haven't thought about that for years."

In the back seat, Luke watched as Sam inhaled a Big Mac in a few bites. He took a big drink, burped, then closed his eyes again. This time he wasn't sleeping. His hands were folded and his lips moved quietly as he prayed.

Paul had the radio tuned to the news. The number of people confirmed dead in Chicago continued to grow. The reporters were talking about the National Guard establishing order. There were warnings about obeying the strict curfew. There were court challenges to the declaration of martial law that would be heard on Monday. The news played a clip of the President saying that until the judges and the ACLU lawyers were willing to pick up a gun and walk the streets of Chicago to keep it safe, he didn't give a damn what their opinion was.

The President was scheduled to speak at a memorial service for the fallen police officers on Monday. The time had been moved up to 2:00 so that people could be home before the curfew. The President would speak at the memorial service and meet with some of the families who had lost loved ones. He would be leaving Chicago Monday night and would not attend the funerals that would start on Tuesday. He told the press that he didn't want to attend the funerals because his security detail and the press would intrude on the families' private time to mourn.

The former President and his wife were still scheduled to speak at the downtown cathedral. They were speaking at a memorial service for some of the Black and Hispanic residents who had been killed in the violence Friday night. It was being billed as a "Unity Event" to help heal the city. Several national politicians were coming to this event, trying to use the national attention to promote themselves. The start time had been moved up to 10:00 a.m., to avoid overlapping the President's event.

Luke's phone buzzed as a text came in.

"Uncle Paul, it's from dad. He's asking if we're okay. He said he texted you a few times and tried to call, but you didn't answer."

"Damn it. I should have let him know about my phone," Paul said. "Can you let him know that my phone is broken and we are about halfway to Chicago?"

"Okay," Luke answered as he texted. "Anything else?" he asked, looking around the car.

"Let him know that we are making good time and I'll call him when we get there. Just that for now," Paul answered.

Luke smiled and sent the text.

CHAPTER 15

Lynn was blowing a bubble. It was getting bigger and bigger, blocking out half of her face before it popped.

She began chewing the gum again, staring at Padre. This was not what he had expected.

"What do you think?" he asked.

They were back in his office, sitting at the same desk where they had watched the speeches on TV the day before. She was sitting with her arms crossed.

"What do I think? I think you are completely full of shit!" She chewed the gum harder as she continued. "I think that everything you just told me is a lie. I think it's bullshit that you don't trust me to help with this. I expected more from you! I THINK you are PISSING ME OFF!"

She glared without talking for several seconds. She continued to chew the gum furiously.

"I can tell by looking at you, and by the absurd story that you gave me, that you've already planned your response to last night. And you have something big planned, so big that you would lie to my face about it. You think you are protecting me by keeping it from me. I don't want your protection. In case you haven't noticed, I have been kicking ass on the street. I have never failed at a job you gave me, EVER! Whatever you're going to do, I can help you, and you know it. I want in."

She continued to glare and chew her gum.

I knew I couldn't fool her, Padre thought to himself, with a touch of pride. He would have been disappointed in her if she hadn't seen right through his lie.

"Friday night was bad," Lynn continued, her voice softening a little. "I know that watching the footage of that violence is hard on men like you, men who want to go fix everything and fix it right now. By the way, I love that about you. I know that you still think of yourself as a warrior, protecting the weak, even in that wheelchair. You should think of yourself that way, because that is who you are. It's what you were born to do. And now you have a very big plan to fix this mess, and I bet it's a good one. Padre, let me help you."

"Let's say you're right," Padre told her. "If I was planning something big like that, it would be a suicide mission, literally. In twenty-four hours, if everything goes according to plan, I will be dead. You are young, Lynn. It would be a waste to see your life end at this point. I'm old, and I haven't taken care of myself like I should have. I've developed sores that won't heal because I won't lie in bed all day. I'm going to end up having amputations and infections. I'm dying in slow motion here. You are just hitting your prime. I don't want you going down with me."

"Do you remember when we first met?" Lynn asked him. They hadn't talked about this in a long time. Her glaring eyes had softened as much as they could. There was a coldness in those eyes that would never completely go away. "I was a scared, pissed off kid feeling helpless. You gave me a choice. You showed me how to fight back. You showed me that I could do good things with my life and make our world better, safer from the predators. You showed me I could choose not to be a victim anymore. I felt dead when I was fourteen. Then you showed up and gave me back my life. You are the only person who has ever believed in me. I'm going with you. You know that I can help. I know that we won't come back. I'm okay with that."

Don't do it, part of his brain warned. *Don't tell her. Don't take her with you. Don't let her die.* Another part of his brain was remembering how she looked when she was just a kid. He was going to do what he had done back then. He would give her a choice. Whatever she decided would be okay with him, but she deserved to hear what he was planning, and then decide for herself. It was the right thing to do.

"That speech from the ex-president was tough to hear. During that speech, I realized that the people, and the ideas, that weaken this country are going to be back in power again. You know how much damage they did the last time around. I think we have moved beyond the tipping point. There are more people willing to vote to weaken our military, open our borders, and bankrupt this country, than there are people who will vote and fight for freedom. Even with the killing that just happened in Chicago, they will somehow twist that as a reason to handcuff the cops and waste more money. They will try to convince people that the system is the reason all those people were killed. They will tell people that we need to understand the criminals, not put them in jail.

My plan is to cut the head off this snake. I plan to kill the former President, his wife, and all the political big shots that will be with him at these funerals. I need to kill all those people to protect this country. They are like locusts. They will keep ravaging this country until the day they die. I have decided that they will die tomorrow. I will kill them, but I won't make it back from this. I wish there were another way, but I don't see any other way to protect this country.

I plan to use the confusion of the Friday night violence, combined with the old, crippled cop routine, to get close to those people at the memorial services on Monday. I have enough C4 in this wheelchair to kill everyone within a quarter mile of the blast. No one else knows this plan. It's my last mission. I'm going to Chicago to die, to keep the enemies of this country from getting back into power. Do you still want in?"

"I'm already packed," Lynn told him. "When do we leave?"

CHAPTER 16

SUNDAY NIGHT

Luke received a group text from Nate when they were an hour outside of Chicago. Nate's leg was broken, and he was being sent to Milwaukee for surgery. He had been trying to help free people who were trapped in a building that had partially collapsed. The building was unstable, and a wall had fallen on him, breaking his leg. The hospitals were so overcrowded that he was being transferred to Milwaukee to have surgery.

After his injury, Nate told the people at the shelter to go to Lincoln Park for safety. There were rumors circulating that it would be a night of more burning and shooting.

"What do we do now?" Luke asked his uncle.

"I don't know," Paul answered. He was back to thinking that they should have stayed home. None of this was going according to plan.

After a pause, Sam answered from the back seat.

"I think you're supposed to go with us," Sam told them. "I think God sent you here to help us. We have come here to tell people who Jesus is, and what He has done for us. I think that there is still more killing ahead for this city, a lot more killing. I think that we might be the last hope for some of these people to hear the truth and be saved."

There was silence when he finished.

"Count me in," Luke told him, breaking the silence. "I'll help any way I can. Just tell me what to do."

Sam held out a massive fist in the back seat. It was unexpected, and it took Luke a moment to realize what he was doing. Luke smiled and fist-bumped him.

"My man," Sam said in his hoarse whisper-voice. "It's good to have you with us."

"Are you sure?" Paul asked him.

In the mirror he could see Luke shake his head yes. "Okay. We're in," Paul said. "So where do we go now?"

"Lincoln Park," Sam answered. "Get us to Lincoln Park."

Two hours later, Paul, Luke, Sam, and JD were standing at the edge of Lincoln Park. It was an unbelievable scene. They had walked past blocks of burned buildings, some just smoking mounds of rubble. They could smell burned flesh as they walked along. Tanks and armored personnel carriers were stationed at the main intersections. Young men with semi-automatic rifles were clustered near their vehicles. Their nervous eyes continued to scan the buildings for snipers. Snipers and IEDs had killed a few of the soldiers, and the news of this had them all on edge. Their guns were trained on Paul's small group as they made their way through the streets. When they saw the soldiers, all four of them would walk with their hands raised in the air to show that they were not armed. Their car had been abandoned more than a mile from the park. Most of the streets were blocked by burned cars and debris from destroyed buildings, making it impossible to drive all the way to the park. They had parked the car in the corner of a parking garage, trying to hide it behind a large, economy van. After two blocks, JD's limp worsened, and the group slowed.

After another block of walking this way, Sam turned to JD and stopped.

"We need to move faster," he said in his raspy whisper. "They are serious about keeping people off the streets once it's dark."

JD nodded and let his friend pick him up like a child and place him on his shoulders.

"Let's go," Sam told them as he started back at a faster pace. It was getting close to sunset. They were stopped at an intersection by a group of six National Guard soldiers as they walked through the quiet streets.

"We have friends and family in the park," JD told the young lieutenant, who was trying to act brave. "We are unarmed. If you want to search us, I certainly understand. It's been a tough few days. I appreciate what you are doing to try to get things back to normal. I've been injured and my big friend is helping me get to the park."

The young man told one of the privates to frisk them. After a cursory pat-down, they were sent on their way, with a warning to get off the streets soon. They could be shot on sight if they were seen traveling after dark. JD thanked the lieutenant for the warning, and they were off at an even faster pace. They were now traveling at a slow jog. As he bounced along at this faster pace, JD winced in pain and held his right hip to try to lessen the pain. Sam slowed the pace to try to ease his friend's pain.

"Thank you for thinking of me," JD told his friend, patting his large shoulder. "Keep focused on what is important here. Get moving. The sun will be down soon."

Sam went back to a slow jog. They were all frisked again as they traveled the last block. Then they were at the edge of the park. The carnage they had seen walking through the streets of Chicago, and the news reports they had heard in the car, hadn't prepared them for the sheer number of injured, dejected, newly homeless people that filled the park. As far as Paul's foursome could see, to the north and to the south, refugees from the violence filled the park. There was an eerie quietness that hung over the park. Some of the people were quietly crying. Some were sitting silently, staring at the ground or watching the main road into camp.

The foursome paused at the start of the main road that led into camp. The road curved to the north and led to a cluster of trailers that had been hastily placed in the park the day before. These trailers served as a command center for the National Guard/Homeland Security. A few medical tents were set up on the far side of the trailers. On the south side of the trailers was a large mobile kitchen. Scores of picnic tables were spread out around the kitchen. Most of the tables were still occupied. People had finished eating, but many stayed at the tables. Some felt safer being close to the command center, others were watching the road into camp, hoping to see loved ones that they hadn't seen since the violence began. Some of the people at the tables simply had no other place to go.

The strangest thing about the camp was the quietness; it felt smothering. The voices from the camp were hushed, sounding like the softer voices people would use in church or at a funeral home. Everyone was suffering some kind of loss – family, friends, pets, a place to call home. There was no laughter in the camp, just shocked faces that were still having trouble coming to terms with the recent loss they had experienced.

"Look at them, brother," JD said quietly to Sam. His voice was hoarse and low as he tried to hold back tears. "They look so hopeless and desperate and sad. Sam, put me down."

The big man glanced up at his friend.

"You sure?" he asked.

"I'm going to limp into that camp, in pain and homeless, just like all these other people. I don't think they will listen to me the same way if they don't see that."

Sam lowered his friend to the ground. JD continued to lean on him for support as they slowly made their way into camp. Paul and Luke followed them. They talked in hushed tones as the mood of the camp settled over them.

The group of newly homeless people staying in Lincoln Park was still stunned and trying to process this new situation. A primitive part of the brain, that had helped people survive for centuries, had them placing every new person that walked into this camp in one of two categories: threat or not a threat. The police and Guard soldiers were just as stunned and were also sorting everyone they saw into one of those two basic categories. To them, these four men looked like potential trouble. No women or children were traveling with them –

a bad sign. The big, white guy had obvious prison tattoos and was as big as a horse. These were definitely men to keep a close eye on.

A loud speaker would occasionally blast information that could be heard throughout the park. As JD limped into the park, the announcements were repeated, first in English, then in Spanish.

> NO WEAPONS ARE ALLOWED IN THE PARK. IF A WEAPON IS FOUND, YOU WILL BE ARRESTED.
>
> DINNER WILL STOP BEING SERVED IN ONE HOUR. BREAKFAST WILL START BEING SERVED AT SUNRISE. BOTTLED WATER IS AVAILABLE OUTSIDE THE COMMAND CENTER ALL DAY AND ALL NIGHT. TAKE ONLY ONE BOTTLE PER PERSON.
>
> COTS AND BLANKETS ARE AVAILABLE AT THE RED CROSS TENTS.
>
> PATROLS WILL BE WALKING THROUGH THE PARK ALL NIGHT. REPORT ANY PROBLEMS TO THE SOLDIERS. ANYONE CAUSING A PROBLEM WILL BE ARRESTED. IF YOU RESIST, YOU MAY BE SHOT.

When the announcements finished, it seemed even quieter.

They had reached the end of the road. The smell of food from the kitchen made Paul's stomach growl and reminded him that it was time for dinner.

"Let's get some food," JD said to the group, as he limped toward the kitchen.

After being served a sack lunch and a bottle of water, they made their way to an empty picnic table. Sam folded his hands as they sat down at the picnic table. The others folded their hands and bowed their heads.

"Father," Sam said in his scratchy voice. "Thank You for this food. Thank You for the chance to be here. Please keep us close to You and help us to be strong enough to obey You. Amen."

Then they were silent as the hungry foursome attacked their dinner. After he finished eating, Luke took out his phone and began recording the scene around the picnic table.

"Smile, everyone," Luke said to his traveling companions as he panned the scene in the park.

"What are you doing?" JD asked.

"The guys who couldn't come on the trip asked me to live stream shots from Chicago. They wanted to be here to see all of this and to help. So this is to show them what's going on. You don't get a real feel for how big this is from TV."

Paul waved at the camera and took the last bite of his sandwich. As he looked around at the other tables, Paul noticed that some of the National Guard soldiers had shifted their position and moved closer to their table.

"It looks like we're getting extra attention from the soldiers," Paul said quietly.

Sam and JD had noticed it too. They expected the attention. Sam shrugged his big shoulders. "What do you expect?" Sam asked him. "We look like criminals."

That comment broke the tension and made them all laugh. The laughter seemed too loud in the quiet park. People at the picnic tables glanced at the unexpected laughter, then most went back to watching the road into the camp.

JD looked around at the tables near them. A large, older black woman a few tables away was staring at him with a look of contempt. She had been rocking and singing softly to herself when the men sat down. She had paused her singing as she sized up the new arrivals. She recognized the crude tattoos as prison tattoos, and categorized JD and Sam as ex-cons who couldn't be trusted. JD smiled and nodded at her. She angrily folded her arms and looked away.

Two young, African-American boys sat at the table next to them. They looked like brothers. They had been watching the road that led into camp, hoping to see family and friends that they had been separated from during the Friday night violence. The older boy glanced at the foursome when they sat down, then went back to watching the road. The younger one continued to stare at Sam.

"He's a strange looking guy, isn't he?" JD asked the younger boy. His voice carried in the quiet camp.

The boy looked at JD and nodded his head yes.

"My name is JD. That strange looking, huge, white dude is Sam. He's my best friend. This guy is Paul and that's his nephew Luke. We just met them today on our way here. They seem like good people. What's your name?" JD asked the boy.

"My name is D'Anthony," the boy said. "This is my brother Leroy."

Leroy pretended to ignore them and kept his eyes on the road.

"It's nice to meet you, D'Anthony," JD told him. His loud voice carried across the whole picnic area. JD limped over to the next table to shake D'Anthony's hand. The large black woman glared at him as he talked to the young boy. "It's good to have a brother, isn't it? It's especially good on a tough day like this. I had a brother when I was growing up, but he was shot and killed. Do you want to hear a crazy story? If you have time, I can tell you an amazing story about how God gave me another brother. Sam here is the new brother God put in my life. He's great, but I still miss my other brother."

"How can he be your brother?" D'Anthony asked him, pointing at Sam.

Paul was interested in hearing that story too. JD was a natural, an amazing public speaker who had the attention of everyone at the surrounding tables. JD sensed the growing interest from the people around him, and raised his voice. This is what he had come to do.

"I'm glad you asked that," JD said, smiling at the young boy. He limped back to his table and stood behind Sam, placing a hand on his friend's big shoulder for support. "D'Anthony, I am a criminal. I'm not proud of it, but I'm not going to lie to you. I spent the last twenty years of my life in prison. When I was young, I was in a gang. I did a lot of bad stuff. I finally got caught and went to jail. In prison, I kept doing all the stupid things that got me in trouble in the first place. I was still in a gang. I kept doing drugs. I even got in trouble with my own gang, and they tried to kill me."

"Did they shoot you?" D'Anthony asked. "Leroy's friend, Thomas, was shot last summer in front of our building. He got shot in the leg."

Leroy had looked away from the road. Both boys were listening to JD's story. Luke continued to live stream to his friends back home as JD spoke. Paul, and the people sitting at the picnic tables around him, were quietly watching JD, eager to hear his answer.

"They didn't have a gun. Three guys tried to beat me to death. One guy was choking me, and the other two guys were hitting me. They got me on the ground and started stomping on me. I should have died, but along came Sam," JD patted his friend on the back. Sam glanced at the growing crowd of people listening to his friend, then went back to staring down at the table. His hands were folded, and his lips were moving as he quietly prayed.

"He saved my life," JD continued "He fought those guys off and kept me safe. For the rest of the time we were in prison together, Sam was there, looking out for me. Sam worked in the infirmary. That's the prison hospital. It's nothing fancy, and the doctors didn't seem to care much about the prisoners. But it was the place where I found the truth and became a Christian. I was stuck in the infirmary for three months. When those men were beating me, they broke some of my ribs, broke my left arm, and some bones in my right hip. It never healed right, and now it hurts every time I walk on that leg."

JD scanned the crowd as he continued. "The doctors said my broken hip had what they called an acetabular fracture. That means that if this is my leg bone that goes into my hip," he held up his left arm, bent his wrist forward, and made a fist. "The broken bone is the part of my hip that the leg goes into." He cupped his left fist with his right hand to demonstrate the leg going into his broken hip socket. Then he was back to leaning on Sam's big shoulder.

"The doctors told me not to put any weight on my leg until they said it was okay. Every two weeks, they would take more x-rays to see if it was healed. It was two months before I could limp around on my leg. Sam here, he brought me food and my pain medicine when it was time. He helped me get dressed, and he helped me stand and pivot to the toilet. It was rough."

"Damn!" D'Anthony said. "They messed you up."

Paul looked up and realized that the crowd had continued to grow while JD spoke. There had been a self-segregation present in the park. North of the command center were predominantly Hispanic families, south of the command center were predominantly Black families. White families were in the middle and stayed clustered closer to the command center. They had taken a strip of land that ran from the command center to some of the big tents the Guard had placed near Lake Michigan.

The crowd was growing, but it was also changing. Several Hispanic families who had been clustered at tables farther away from JD had moved closer and were listening to him and talking to each other in Spanish. JD stood up on the picnic table bench so that the crowd could see him better. He looked unsteady, trying to balance on the bench.

"I need help, brother," he said quietly to Sam.

Sam nodded and stood on the ground next to his friend. JD reached down and continued to lean on Sam's big shoulder to support himself. Sam continued to stare down at the picnic table and pray silently.

"Come on closer," JD said to the growing crowd, his voice becoming even louder as he continued. Luke stood up and panned the crowd, then focused his phone back on JD as he continued to live-stream. "I want everyone to hear my story. It is a true story with a happy ending. The best part is that at the very end, which hasn't happened yet, we get to live happily ever after! That's right boys," he told D'Anthony and Leroy. "Happily ever after."

This guy is amazing, Paul thought as he listened to JD. In five minutes, he had the attention of everyone at the parks new dining area.

"I'm going to start over, for all of you who didn't hear me when I was talking with my new friends, D'Anthony and Leroy here."

"My name is J.D. White," JD told the growing crowd. "I grew up in Kansas City in a rough neighborhood. I dropped out of school and became a criminal at an early age. I joined a gang, and I did a lot of bad stuff. I was caught by the police several times, and eventually I ended up in jail. I spent the last twenty years of my life in prison. When I got put in prison, I was still in a gang, still doing drugs, still doing the same stupid things that got me in trouble. That life was all I knew. I think that sometimes, people keep making the same stupid mistakes because it's all they know.

Well, I let my big mouth get me into a lot of trouble when I was in jail, and one day three guys got me alone, and they were beating me to death. I'm on the ground, not even able to fight back. I'm trying to curl up in a ball to protect myself, and they were stomping on me. I thought I was gonna die, and to tell you the truth, I wasn't at all surprised that this was how my life would end. I was trying to cover my face while they were beating me, and the craziest part is that I wasn't yelling for help. I was yelling out in pain when they got in a good shot, but I didn't yell for help, because I knew that nobody cared, and nobody was gonna come help me. That day was the most alone I ever felt. I had been in fights, and I had been shot at, but there was always somebody who might help me if I yelled out. That day, when I realized that it wouldn't do any good to yell out, 'cause nobody was gonna help me, man, that lonely feeling was almost as bad as the beating."

JD paused and took a big drink from his water. He did a half turn to the left and to the right, trying to look at everyone in the crowd before he continued. The edge of the crowd continued to fill in with more people from all parts of the camp. Camera crews from the networks had seen the crowd grow and were now broadcasting live from the picnic tables. JD's bad leg started to buckle as he stood on the picnic table bench. He would have fallen if he hadn't been leaning on Sam.

"Brother," he told Sam. "I need more help."

Sam nodded his head. He picked up JD and placed him on his broad shoulders.

"So far, that's not a very happy bedtime story, is it?" JD asked the growing crowd. "Like I said, I'm lying there, thinking I'm gonna die, and suddenly nobody is beating me anymore. I heard some strange noises, and then it's quiet. I had blood in my eyes, and I couldn't see. When I finally wiped all that blood out of my eyes and looked around, there was Sam. I knew who he was, but I don't think I had ever talked to him. He looked around to make sure that nobody else was gonna jump in. Then he knelt down next to me and asked me where I was hurt. When he saw that I couldn't walk, he picked me up and carried me to the infirmary. I was bleeding, I mean I was dripping blood on the floor, leaving a trail. Thank God we were close to the infirmary, so we didn't have far to go. He put me on a cot and told the nurse there to get a doctor and that my right hip is probably broken, and that I had some cuts on my head and arm that needed to get stitched up. Now the same guards, who didn't seem to care that I was getting beaten to death, showed up because of the trail of blood, and they had guns on me and Sam. He lay down and put his hands on his head. They cuffed him and the guards took him away. A few days later, he was back at his job in the infirmary. He brought me food and helped me every time I needed to stand and get to a toilet. He brought me stuff to wash up and to brush my teeth. His job was to clean the floors and make the beds in the infirmary, but I saw him doing so much more for everybody there who was hurt.

The guard who worked in the infirmary on weekdays was this nice old guy named Dennis. He had a radio on his desk, and every morning he had it on Bott radio, that's a Christian radio station. It broadcasts all of these different preachers. They had some great teachers on that station, guys like David Jeremiah and John McArthur, Alistair Begg, and Michael Youssef, and my personal favorite, Tony Evans. Each day I get a chance to hear some real Christian teaching. I had never really heard people teach from the Word of God. I didn't think too much of it at first, but I kept watching this huge, gentle man help me and the other criminals in the infirmary. Don't let anybody fool you, there are no innocent men in prison. All of them deserve to be there. Most of them should never be let back out into the real world or they will just hurt more people. But Sam here, he helped everybody."

JD paused to take another quick drink from his water bottle. He continued to scan the crowd, hoping to see his words working in the hearts of these frightened people. Both Leroy and D'Anthony were done watching the road. Their eyes were fixed on JD. He glanced back down at the two boys and smiled.

"This is the best part, boys," he said, then he was back to addressing the crowd.

"I realized that I needed to change my life. I had that thought before, but I never changed. But this time, I really wanted to be different. I wanted to be like Sam. I was watching somebody who was different from anybody I had ever known. And each day, the Bible teaching I was listening to on the radio was helping to open my eyes. Sam didn't push his beliefs on me. He was more a man of action than a talker. When I asked him what changed his life, he answered with just one word – Jesus. That's all he said – Jesus.

So I started reading the Bible when I was lying in that bed with my broken hip. I asked Dennis, the guard, if I could have one, and right away, he gave me the Bible that was on his desk. It had all these highlighted areas and notes written on the side. One of the teachers on the radio had been teaching from John 3. He called John 3:16 the greatest verse in the Bible. For those of you who don't know this one, it is when one of the Jewish leaders is talking to Jesus at night. Jesus tells him that God loves us so much, that He sent Jesus into the world, not to condemn people, but so that we could all be saved by believing in Him. It seems like an easy thing to believe, that God might love the whole world, but then the preacher I was listening to broke it down, and said, 'put your name into that sentence'. So instead of just saying God loved the whole world so much that He sent Jesus as a sacrifice for our sins, I read the sentence this way: For God loved me so much, He loved JD White, a no-good drug dealing gang banger so much, that He sent His one and only Son, Jesus, into the world to die, to pay for MY sins, so that if I believe in him, I shall not perish, but..." JD paused to choke back tears that were forming. "But I will be able to live forever in heaven with the God who LOVES ME. But if I DO NOT believe in Him, I stand condemned to spend eternity in hell, because I HAVE NOT believed in Jesus, and my sins ARE NOT forgiven.

It seems too easy, doesn't it? There just has to be more that I have to do to earn it, but there's not. That's it. Believe in Jesus as your very own personal Savior, and you are saved. That's what separates true Christianity from all the other religions. Every other religion will tell you that you need to do more good things than bad things, and if you do enough, then you can earn forgiveness. The Bible says that none of us will do enough good stuff EVER to earn our salvation, but the good news is that we don't have to – Jesus did all the hard work, we just need to believe."

He paused again to let his words sink in.

"At first, I thought that God should not forgive me. It didn't seem right. I had done so many awful things, I couldn't really believe that God would love me and want to forgive ME. But Dennis showed me the parts in the Bible that say that when I was at my very worst, God loved me, and that He always will. And nothing can separate me from the love of my Father. If you have done bad things, I mean very bad things that you are ashamed of, you may think that what you did is so bad that God won't forgive you. The good news for everyone who feels that way, is that YOU ARE WRONG! God loves you and wants to forgive you, right now.

So here's what I want you to do," he told them. "I want you to put your name in that beautiful sentence. God loves you so much D'Anthony, or Leroy, or Sam, or whoever you are, that He sent His Son to die and take the punishment for your sins, so that you could be forgiven and spend forever with the God who loves you. Do it, put your name in that sentence."

JD paused and looked out at the murmuring crowd. Some had folded their hands and were quietly praying. Some of the people in the crowd were crying, others were angrily arguing with the people near them. Night had come while JD talked. The few bright lights that had been set up in the park cast shadows across the picnic tables.

Paul had listened to some amazing Christian teachers. He knew the truth that JD was teaching, but he had never seen such a dynamic speaker in person. He felt so fortunate to be sitting here, listening to JD preach in the park. Paul had teared up repeatedly while he listened to JD. *Thank You, Father*, he quietly prayed, *for letting me be here tonight. Thank you for letting me help get these men to Chicago, so they could spread the Word to all these hopeless people.*

JD's small break was over. He was back to teaching.

"I don't know how saying that verse makes you feel, but it made me cry. The Bible says in the first chapter of the Gospel of John, that for those who believe in the name of Jesus, they have become children of God. I knew for sure that I was a sinner, separated from God by all the sin in my life, and I would never be able to make things right by what I did. But I learned that I could accept the amazing gift of Jesus being crucified as punishment for all my sins, so I could be forgiven, and one day I would spend forever with God in heaven. The Bible says that as soon as I believed, His Spirit started living in me. As soon as I believed, I was born again as A LOVED CHILD OF GOD!"

JD paused again. He held his arms above his head in victory with his fists clenched. Many in the crowd were clapping and cheering for him. He took another drink of his water and scanned the crowd before speaking again. His gaze finally came to rest on D'Anthony and Leroy at the table next to him. He smiled and winked at the boys. He held up his hands to quiet the crowd and continued.

"I have memories of doing some really bad things. Some of those awful things I did, I was proud of back when I did them, 'cause I thought it made me look tough. But I've got all these bad memories and regrets stuck in my head. Sometimes, those memories create doubts, and undermine my faith. Here's the bad news about believing in Jesus. When you become a child of God, you have made a new enemy. That's right, there is a devil who is now my enemy, and he will attack in all kinds of ways. One of the ways he attacks me is by trying to get me to focus on old habits, old ways of seeing the world and myself, and how I fit into it all. I sometimes still have moments when doubt creeps in, and I think that I'll never amount to anything, that nobody will like me if they know what I've done, that I don't deserve to be forgiven. All that doubt will come at me in little waves, and sometimes in big crashing waves. When those attacks come at me, and they do when I'm feeling weak, I have learned to hold onto the truth. The truth I hold tight to is that there is an awesome, powerful, loving God, who sent His Son to die for MY sins, and for YOUR sins. The awesome truth is that I have accepted this gift, and I am now a child of God, and I can NEVER be separated from the love of my Father."

He paused briefly and wiped the tears from his eyes. Sam could hear him sniffling. The big man patted JD's leg for encouragement and continued to pray for his friend as he preached.

"You're doing good," Sam told his friend.

"Please listen to me!" JD yelled at the murmuring crowd. "The time to make the biggest decision of your life is running out! The most important question you will ever be asked is 'Who is Jesus Christ?' Is He your personal Savior? Did he die for YOUR sins so that YOU could become a child of God and one day be united with your loving Father in heaven? I had time to slowly learn the truth about God when I was hurt. The bad news I'm telling you is that YOU ARE RUNNING OUT OF TIME! You may not want to believe me, but it's true. A week ago, you wouldn't have believed me if I told you that you'd be camped out in Lincoln Park with thousands of other people. A week ago, you wouldn't have believed me if I had said that your buildings would be burned to the ground and the National Guard would be in charge of this city.

Believe me when I say that the violence in this city is not over! THE TIME IS SHORT! Do not count on having months to think this over. Pray about this tonight. Repent and turn your hearts to God! Accept Jesus as your personal Savior before it is too late. Remember, to NOT make a decision is still MAKING a decision. Open your hearts to the truth! Ask God to open your eyes and your hearts, 'cause very soon it will be too late!"

J.D. paused. The crowd had continued to push closer to him as he talked. He could hear people arguing loudly in Spanish and English. The loudspeaker that had been broadcasting announcements when they first arrived broke in, drowning out the crowd.

> BY ORDER OF THE NATIONAL GUARD AND HOMELAND SECURITY, DISPERSE AND RETURN TO YOUR COTS. A CURFEW HAS

BEEN ORDERED. LARGE GATHERINGS ARE NOT ALLOWED IN THE PARK AFTER DARK. PLEASE LEAVE THE DINING AREA AND RETURN TO YOUR COTS IN AN ORDERLY FASHION.

The message was then given in Spanish. JD couldn't be heard over the loudspeakers. He waited for the announcement to stop, but it didn't. It was repeated again in English and Spanish. Police officers on horseback were coming toward JD. More National Guard soldiers were appearing near the picnic tables in groups of two and three. One of the armored vehicles was inching closer to the group of picnic tables.

JD watched, stunned, as the crowd broke up and started drifting away.

"Sam, I don't understand," JD said bewildered. "That's what we were supposed to do, wasn't it? I was ready to preach all night. I don't get it. What did I do wrong?"

JD was still sitting on the big man's shoulders. Sam watched the crowd that was breaking up and slowly leaving. The big man shrugged his shoulders in response to the question from his friend.

At the closest picnic table, Leroy stood up. He took one last look at the road leading into the camp. "Come on, D," he told his brother. "We're supposed to go."

D'Anthony was still watching JD and Sam. He stood up to leave with his brother. He gave a small wave before walking away. Sam waved back. He could see the large woman, who had looked away from JD when they first sat down, following close behind them. Then the National Guard Soldiers were blocking his view of the boys. The soldiers coming closer to the foursome at the picnic table had their rifles out, but pointed down at the ground for safety. The message was clear. This was the first group of soldiers Paul had seen in camp that looked ready to use their rifles. The Guardsmen were young, and most of them looked scared. Paul noticed that Luke was still live-streaming all of this to his friends.

"Come with us," the command was directed at JD and Sam. The soldier in front, who had given the command, was gripping his rifle tight. He was talking much louder than needed. He looked like he was only a few years older than Luke. He was a tall, athletic looking kid, probably doing this for college money, Paul thought to himself. Now he's scared and doesn't want his friends to see it. The young man's gun had started to rise as he neared the group. It was now pointed at Sam.

Sam and JD knew right away what they were dealing with. They had seen plenty of new guards at the prison. It seemed like they had all been given the same speech. Don't act scared even though you obviously are. Talk in your loud voice and use implied threats of violence to show them who's in charge.

"You see my hands," JD said, showing the young man his empty palms, trying to keep him calm. "My friend here is going to put me down, nice and slow. We were frisked walking into the camp, but I'm sure you'll want to do that again, just to be on the safe side. Then we'll go wherever you want. I have a bad hip, so I might move slow, but I'll keep right on moving with you. Isn't that right, Sam?"

Sam nodded his head yes as he placed his friend on the ground. Then both men placed their hands on their heads and stood with their legs apart, waiting to be frisked. It seemed to work. The young soldier pointed his gun down at the ground again. The volume of his voice had returned to a normal level as he spoke to one of his men, telling him to frisk Sam and JD.

"Corporal, what about them?" one of the soldiers asked as he pointed toward Paul and Luke.

"You two, don't move," the corporal barked at Paul and Luke. He had gone back to using his louder, I'm-in-control voice. He turned back to the soldier who had asked the original question. "Frisk them too. The Homeland Security Agent wants to talk to all of them."

CHAPTER 17

Marco had fallen asleep. After dry heaving all day, he had fallen asleep just before sunset. Between jet lag and being sea sick, he could not remember ever feeling so miserable. He had returned to his dream of the hero's parade down the main street of his hometown. He was in the back of the flatbed truck again, waving to the adoring crowd. The dream ended abruptly as yells of protest from the boat's crew, followed by gunfire, rang out in the boat. Marco rolled over on his bunk. He had been facing the wall when he fell asleep. When he rolled over onto his other side, he could see out of the bedroom door into the ship's small galley. The ship's two crew members had been sitting at the table eating the dinner that Antonio had prepared. They had been shot in the chest as they ate their pasta. They had fallen out of their chairs and lay on the floor with blood spreading around them. Antonio took the bodies and moved them into the bedroom where Marco had been sleeping. He placed them against the back wall, stacking them on top of each other.

Marco didn't talk while Antonio moved the bodies. When Antonio finished, he dished himself up a plate of pasta from the stove and placed his food on the table in the bedroom with Marco and the corpses. He didn't eat in the ship's galley because of the mess he had made when he killed the two men.

"Don't we need the crew?" Marco asked. He was hesitant to say anything that might anger Antonio. The threats from earlier that day were more troubling after watching Antonio kill these men, then calmly load up his plate with pasta.

"This boat has a computer system that is much like the automatic pilot that a plane uses. It is programmed to take us to Chicago. We do not need the crew any longer. We were out of cell phone coverage, but we are going to have coverage again as we get closer. I wanted them dead before they could communicate with anyone. It is just a precaution to make sure that there are no surprises as we arrive in Chicago."

Antonio finished his pasta before he spoke again.

"That wasn't bad," he said as he finished eating. Antonio seemed to be in a much better mood. He lit a cigarette after he finished eating. "I can help you feel better tomorrow morning. One more bad night, then we will be close enough that I can give you medicine and IV fluids, and I will have enough to keep you healthy until we are in Chicago. When you feel better, you will have to check and double-check the detonator of the bomb. We will have one chance to do this right. If the police spot us, they will kill us. If they do that before you can detonate the bomb, then this will all have been a waste."

There was a short-wave radio on a shelf next to Antonio. He reached over, turned it on, and turned up its volume. Some static could be heard as the radio was turned on.

"This is how we will communicate with the outside world. We have friends who can use this to reach us if there is a change in the plan. Our phones had to be left in Canada so that we couldn't be tracked. If we need help, we can call out, but this operation should be as dark as possible. That means that we are not supposed to call out unless it is an emergency."

Marco could occasionally hear pieces of conversations coming over the short-wave radio, although he couldn't understand the bits of English and French that could be heard. They rode this way in silence, Marco on the bunk and Antonio smoking near the radio. The short wave suddenly came alive.

> This is the BBC reporting live. We have breaking news from Chicago. There is a gathering in Lincoln Park that the police had to disperse, and there are reports of arrests being made. A group of four men, who have recently been released from prison, were apprehended in the park after making threats of violence. This was recorded earlier this evening near the Illinois National Guard Command Center that has been established in the park.

JD's talk from the picnic tables was broadcast over the radio. Luke's live stream had gone viral on the internet and had been picked up by several news services. Most of the news services had edited JD's comments down to two sentences. 'You are running out of time...B elieve me when I say that the violence in this city is not over.' The two sentences were run together by the media. The news reports would then start going into the criminal history of Sam and JD. The BBC newscast over the shortwave had all night to fill, and the biggest story of the news cycle was the violence in Chicago. They decided to run with the full recording of JD talking at the picnic tables. They even played the recording of the foursome being arrested. It ended when Luke's phone was confiscated by the National Guard.

"It certainly must seem like the world is indeed ending tonight in Chicago, Illinois," the BBC broadcaster added as the tape ended. "Local law enforcement has been struggling to contain this latest surge in gang violence. Imposing a curfew and declaring martial law seem to have turned the tide in that city. Many civil rights groups are threatening to sue the..."

The voice faded into unintelligible static. Antonio reached for the radio and turned down the volume. Marco's angry voice reached him as he lit another cigarette.

"How can they broadcast such blasphemy? This infidel will pay for his proselytizing!"

Antonio was used to the ideas of free speech and religious freedom that the West valued. He had come to expect this reaction of anger from Middle Eastern associates who lived in Muslim countries. He had grown weary of trying to explain the Western way of thinking to these people. He ignored what Marco said and took a long drag on his cigarette. The words of JD continued to play in his head, distracting him from Marco. Then it occurred to him what Marco's words meant.

"How do you know what was said on the radio?" he spoke to Marco's back.

"I have learned of the people of the Book," Marco continued, still angry about what he had heard. "At home, they were occasionally arrested for proselytizing. It is a crime that deserves death. There was a boy from my village who was found listening to tapes with infidel teachings on them. He was beaten by his family as punishment. When he wouldn't renounce his blasphemy, he was turned over to the police and was taken to prison. He died while he was in prison. He was his father's oldest son. He brought such shame upon his family, but his father was honored by the imam at Friday prayers, in front of the whole village, for the way he defended the Faith."

"Do you speak English or Italian?" Antonio asked. He realized that he had heard the broadcast switch back and forth between the two languages.

He spoke while facing Marco's back. He rose and walked toward the bunk, gripping his gun in his right hand. He grabbed Marco's shirt with his left hand and turned the young man to face him.

"Do you understand me? Who are you? What languages do you speak? Why did you hide this from me? Are you a spy for the Americans?" he yelled in English as he pointed the gun at Marco's face. "Answer me or I will shoot you right now!" he commanded, switching to Italian.

"Stop!" Marco pleaded. "I don't understand! Don't shoot me!" His hands were raised defensively in front of his face. He was beginning to cry. All of his answers were in Farsi.

"Look!" Antonio commanded. He turned the gun to show Marco that he was taking off its safety. He pushed the gun against Marco's groin.

"Tell me or I will shoot your balls off," Antonio told him, switching back to English.

"I don't understand what you are saying. Please don't shoot me," Marco pleaded in Farsi.

Antonio lowered the gun, watching the young man cry with fear. After a moment, he turned and left the room. He climbed up to the deck of the ship and watched the moon over the waves. The computer continued to guide them toward Chicago.

He hadn't had any free time in months to sit still like this. There had been so much planning, so many details to worry about. It felt strange to sit and wait, with nothing to do for hours. His mind drifted as he continued to smoke and watch the waves roll by. How could Marco know what was said on the radio? He knew the young man's complete history. He couldn't believe that this man was a double agent. He knew Marco's friends, family, and educational history. He didn't know how this man could have learned English without it being known by the people around him. Something was not right, and Antonio was worried that he could be walking into a trap. If this was a trap, Antonio realized that he was stuck on this boat in the middle of the Great Lakes, with no place to go.

He lit another cigarette and sat down in one of the chairs on the deck. An old song was running through his mind. It was a lullaby his mother used to sing to him. She used to rub his back at night and sing to him as he fell asleep. Antonio had faded, warm memories of his mother. He had trouble remembering her face, but he could remember her soothing voice. She had been a pretty young woman, he knew from pictures. She had died due to complications from her second pregnancy. A blood clot had caused her death. When she was gone, the happy memories of home ended.

He hadn't thought of her in a long time. All this talk of love had stirred up old memories of his mother. She had loved him; he knew that. Then she was suddenly gone, and his life had changed.

After her death, he started spending more time at the local mosque. It helped fill the empty days. His father had been lost in his own grief and didn't have the time or energy for his son. At the mosque, he had met many harsh, unforgiving men with Marco's attitude. All of them would have agreed with Marco that the man on the radio deserved death for teaching against the faith. At one point, he would have agreed with them too. Living in Italy and traveling around the world had mellowed him with time. He was smart enough to keep quiet about his new-found tolerance when he spoke with the people he worked for. He eventually realized that the adults who had been giving him attention and teaching him at the mosque were grooming him to work for The Faith. He was a perfect candidate; no family connections or loyalties to distract him from his job.

Over time, the men at the local mosque were replaced by more powerful men, in bigger mosques, in larger cities. He had been working for them for years. These men were the ones who had told him a year ago that he had been selected to help execute the biggest strike against the infidels that had happened in hundreds of years. The fact that it was a suicide mission had not been explained to Antonio at first. He had originally been told that his job was to transport a scientist, who could not speak English, to the United States to detonate a nuclear weapon. He was also in charge of the logistics of getting a nuclear bomb onto a chartered boat and of leaving no trail that could lead back to the men he worked for. He didn't know if they were serious at first. An action like that would be madness. It would start the next world war.

It had been explained to Antonio that precautions had been taken to blunt the American response. It had also been explained to him that this was not a request; this was now his assignment. He knew what that meant. If he refused, he would be executed. If he tried to run, or tell the Americans, he would be captured, tortured, then executed. He threw himself into planning the details of the most dangerous mission he could have ever imagined. It was a challenge that his sharp mind enjoyed. He doubted that the mission would actually be successful; there were just too many things that could go wrong. Antonio tried not to think about the devastation that would result if he succeeded.

If it is God's will, this will be a success. If this is not God's will, the mission will not be successful, Antonio thought to himself, invoking the fatalistic view of life that he used to lessen his guilt when he thought about the massive death that could occur. This was what he had been taught as a boy when he had searched for answers after his mother's death. When he asked why it was God's will that his mother had died, he had been told harshly not to question the will of God. He had never been satisfied with that answer, but he had learned to keep his doubts to himself. He had been good at suppressing his doubts and staying busy with plans for the next mission, the next challenge. In between planning missions, he spent time vacationing with rich friends. They would travel to some of the nicest cities and most beautiful locations in the world. His cover as a rich Fiat executive had its advantages.

He continued to smoke in silence and watch the moon reflect off the waves. The sight of the moon on the water reminded him of his time relaxing by the Mediterranean. He loved the warm, beautiful water of the Mediterranean. He loved the rocking motion of the water. Years ago, he had fallen in love with one of the women he met there. Her name was Sofia. She was the only woman he had ever been in love with. The happiest days of his life had been with Sofia. He hadn't thought of her in a long time. He had been able to push away those memories by keeping busy with his work. Some nights, those memories would resurface, despite his busy schedule. On those nights, he would use a good Italian wine to drown out the memories.

Tonight, the waves and the moon, and the strange teaching on the radio, reminded him of the only two people who had ever made him feel loved. Tonight he couldn't use a good Italian wine to hide from his memories, or his feelings of loneliness. He wondered where Sofia was, and if she was looking at the same moon tonight. He hoped she was happy. He hoped that she had found someone who loved her and that she had a family. She deserved a life full of happiness and love.

Antonio had been told to leave her. The people he worked for did not have plans for him to marry or have a family. He had reminded his superiors that drinking and being promiscuous were part of his cover in the West. They had given him approval for that lifestyle, but told him to leave the woman he loved. His allegiance was supposed to be to his mission, to advancing the faith the way his handlers defined it. He had thought briefly about running away with Sofia, but he realized that they would be hunted down and killed. In the end, he would not be allowed to walk away from this job, and he would not be able to protect her. He felt sad and alone, staring at the waves. He should have brought wine on this trip.

JD's words kept playing in his head as he watched the water roll by. He had never learned about true Christianity. He knew a little about some of the rituals, festivals, and superstitious beliefs of the local church in his Italian town. It had seemed so silly when he heard of the local customs. Tonight, the teaching he heard didn't seem silly. Tonight, it stirred something deep within him. He realized that he had finished the last cigarette in his pack. To get another pack, he would have to go back to the sleeping quarters below. He didn't want to talk to Marco again. He felt conflicted; it reminded him of how hard it had been to walk away from Sofia such a long time ago.

JD's preaching at the park continued to echo in his brain. The message of a loving God that Antonio had never known became overwhelming. Then, he began speaking quietly to the moon and the waves.

"For God so loved me, Moshen, that He gave His one and only Son, Jesus. So that I can believe in Him, and have eternal life. For God so loved me..."

He began to sob quietly, as he continued to clutch the empty pack of cigarettes.

CHAPTER 18

The guitar notes at the start of the song were beautiful, pure chords. The voice of Meredith Brooks could be heard joining the guitar. Lynn loved the acoustic version of this song. She had earbuds in both ears and had closed her eyes. Her music always helped her relax. This job worried her because there were so many unknowns. It also worried her because it felt so rushed. All the other jobs she had done with Padre had been more carefully planned. She was forcing herself to take a break from planning. It was time to find a peaceful moment.

The words of the song filled her head. The opening line was her favorite: "I hate the world today. You're so good to me, I know but I can't change. Tried to tell you. But you look at me like maybe I'm an angel underneath, Innocent and sweet. Yesterday I cried..."

Her moment of peace ended when the overhead speaker in the ceiling above her started in with an announcement loud enough to drown out the music. She took out the earbuds, giving up on the idea of a peaceful moment.

"Son of a bitch," Padre said angrily. "Did you hear that? The plane is being delayed again."

"It looks like the delay is pissing you off," Lynn said quietly. Her voice was low, but stern. She was sitting at the end of a row of seats at Kansas City International Airport, Terminal B, Gate Thirty-Two. Padre sat next to her in his modified wheelchair, the one loaded with plastic explosives. No one was sitting close enough to hear her speaking to him.

"Here's the fun part," Lynn said sarcastically. "Everyone else knows that you are sitting here pissed off. That fat dimwit at the TSA desk, who keeps trying to look down my dress, knows that you're pissed off. If there was a goddamn four-year old watching you right now, that little kid would know that you are pissed off.

I thought that we were NOT trying to attract attention. You are supposed to look like a weak, tired old cripple who needs my help. I am the eye candy that distracts people. The security idiots in this airport have been on higher alert since Friday night. You are looking, and acting, like a potential threat. I would have my eyes on you if I were security here. You look like you're about to start trouble.

You've been behind your desk and off the street for too many years. You have forgotten how to become invisible. You need to hunch down in that chair. We need to cover up your shoulders and arms with a blanket. You need to put a little shake in your hands, and you need to act weak. The security people in Chicago are going to be on edge and looking for potential problems more than the TSA idiots here. They need to look at you and think that you are harmless. They need to see you as someone who doesn't even deserve a second look."

Lynn dropped her phone intentionally with a loud 'whoops.' She bent to pick the phone off the floor. The TSA agent heard the drop and looked down her dress as she bent to grab the phone.

"Let them see what you want them to see. They are going to make snap judgements based on their first look at you, and they want to feel secure. Work that angle. We want them to see you as a weak, old crippled guy that a pretty, young girl is pushing in a wheelchair. If we do this right, they won't see us as a threat until we blow it all up."

Padre looked down at his hands quietly for a moment, then readjusted his position in the chair. He hunched down lower in his chair and bowed his head.

"You're right," he told her quietly. He was looking down at the floor and sounded angry. Right now, Lynn didn't care if he was angry. This needed to be done right the first time

Padre was upset, but his anger was directed at himself, not at Lynn's correction. He knew she was right. He was mad that she needed to remind him of their cover. How could he be so sloppy? Maybe he had been behind a desk too long. He was glad that Lynn had insisted on going with him. She was so damn smart.

"I saw a shop down the hall where I can buy you a blanket," Lynn told him. "I'll be right back."

The TSA agent looked up from his phone to watch her as she walked away and he watched as she brought the blanket back and placed it over Padre's shoulders. He settled down lower in the chair as Lynn placed a large, light blue Kansas City Royals blanket over his shoulders and arms. There were a few choices at the gift shop. Lynn decided that the light blue looked more passive than the bright red chiefs blanket next to it in the store. She had it up high to cover his large, muscular neck. She had also gotten him a blue baseball cap with KC on the front. She placed it on his head and stepped back to inspect her work. She nodded approvingly at the changes and sat back down next to Padre. Padre's hands shook visibly as he adjusted his new cap.

CHAPTER 19

"Do you think I'm stupid?"

The man asking the question was a short, stocky man with a crew cut. He sat on a chair facing the four prisoners. The prisoners stood in a small holding cell in a Homeland Security trailer with their hands cuffed behind them. It was the size of a trailer that would routinely be placed on a construction site and used as an on-site office by the general contractor. This trailer had been modified by homeland security to act as a mobile jail. The walls had been reinforced with steel, and bars had been placed over the windows. A wall of metal bars separated the trailer into two sections. One third of the trailer became a small jail, with a door in the middle that locked from the outside. The four traveling companions stood in the locked compartment.

The man asking the question sat on the other side of the metal bars, with two Illinois National Guard soldiers standing behind him – one male, one female. He had introduced himself as Agent Anderson from

Homeland Security when he had entered the trailer. He had taken the only chair in the trailer when he started questioning the prisoners. He had seemed angry when he entered the trailer. Thirty minutes had gone by, and he seemed much angrier than when he had started.

"I asked you a question. Do you think I'm stupid?" the crew-cut man asked again as he got off the chair and walked closer to the wall of bars that divided the trailer.

"So, I'm supposed to believe that these two," he said, pointing with two fingers to Luke and Paul, "are driving up here to help out at a local shelter, despite all the killing and burning from Friday night. They just happen to meet you two by chance," he pointed to Sam and JD, "and they agree to give you a ride to Chicago. And then when you have your little revival meeting at the picnic tables, everyone just magically heard you speak in their language. Even the damn Somalis heard you speak in whatever the hell language they speak. They have been raising hell about the infidel teaching about Jesus. If I let you out, they just might slit your throat. I bet that hurts, doesn't it?" he asked as he eyed the scar across the front of Sam's neck.

No one responded to the agent's questions.

"I have all night to get the truth out of you four. I will get it. We might as well do this the easy way," Anderson said, letting his implied threat sink in.

"All right," he said, as his gaze moved from prisoner to prisoner. "Let's start over. You two" – he pointed again at Sam and JD – "get out of jail yesterday in Kansas and decide to come to Chicago to teach about God. So, you are here tonight, telling people that they are not safe, that more death and destruction will rain down from above.

When I ask you how you know this, you tell me that God shows the big guy what's going to happen in his dreams.

That sounds like total bullshit to me. Here's your future the way I see it. You are going back to jail. We have you two on parole violations. That's right. You got out of jail and crossed two state lines without telling your parole officer. I have you causing a disturbance here, and I can dream up more charges to put you back in prison.

You two," he pointed at Luke and Paul, "are in trouble for transporting these two across state lines, for causing a disturbance, and like I said, I can come up with more reasons to put you in jail. But I don't want you four in jail here. I want you to tell me the truth about what you know, and then I want you to go back to Kansas City. This little refugee camp, for lack of a better term, has been quiet and peaceful. I will not have anybody getting these people worked up. Most of them have lost loved ones, and they are sad, but some of them are starting to get angry.

I want people in this camp who will calm that anger down. There is a large tent close to the lake that is our chapel, temple, whatever the hell kind of church you want it to be. We have been rotating local priests, rabbis, imams, and Buddhists in that tent trying to help people cope. None of THEM are telling these people that worse things are coming. They are talking to people about peace and love and forgiveness and karma, some version of cosmic bullshit connecting all of the good and bad in the universe. But I'm supposed to believe that God is talking to you guys, and not to those religious people?"

He looked at the four men in the cell, waiting for a response. JD wouldn't look up at the Homeland Security agent. He kept staring down at his feet, looking defeated, the complete opposite of the man who had been so animated at the picnic table just a short time ago. The others stood quietly, facing Agent Anderson.

"We told you the truth," Sam finally told him in his scratchy, whisper voice. "I know that you're doing your job, but we need to get back out there and keep teaching. This is very important. We don't have much time."

"You keep saying that, but I don't believe you," Anderson answered. "I think that if real trouble was coming, you would have stayed in Kansas. I bet that you know a lot more than you are telling me. I think you heard something in prison about all of this, and now you are here to cash in. I think your angle is to predict the future, look like a prophet getting information straight from God, then start asking for donations. You won't have to steal money from these people, they will be dumb enough to give you their money if you make them feel safe. You can get rich, and it's not illegal, very smart."

Agent Anderson pulled folded papers from his back pocket and held them up as he unfolded them.

"How in the world can I be so cynical? Why would I ever think that you two are dirtballs lying to people to take their money?" the agent asked Sam and JD. "Maybe your friends don't understand who they decided to give a ride to. Let's enlighten them with your arrest records.

For JD, 'the Man of God', you've been arrested over a dozen times. You have been nailed multiple times for possession, possession with intent to sell, assault, aggravated assault, robbery, battery, arson, disturbing the peace, obstructing an officer, resisting arrest, and finally murder.

For Sam, the Dream Prophet, multiple counts of rape, aggravated sodomy, assault, and of course, murder.

But the fun doesn't end there. The good Dr. Paul Davidson was convicted of assaulting a patient. That one got your medical license suspended. Ouch. Well, I'm sure that the patient was asking for it, right, Doc?" he asked.

He paused, waiting to see if anyone in the group would respond. He was met with continued silence.

"This is the wrong group to be hanging out with," Anderson told Luke. "You seem to be a model student, and you don't get into any trouble. You are a minor, so we are contacting your father. You will remain in our custody until we get you back to your father."

"You two are back under arrest," his attention was back on Sam and JD. "We are asking the police in Kansas to come pick you up and take you back to prison for violating your parole. The sooner we get you out of this city, the better. We have the President, the former President, and all these big shots flying in here. They get here tonight, and they will speak at wakes and funerals tomorrow. If it were up to me, I would keep the political clowns out of this city until we have a chance to restore order, but it's not up to me. So they are coming, and you four are going, real soon. You should all be on your way out of here before breakfast. Watching you leave will be a relief. I don't need people causing trouble in this camp."

"Sir," Sam said in his raspy voice, "I'm sorry. We should have asked you if it was okay to address that crowd at the picnic tables. The stuff you just read about us is true, but it's who we were, and what we did years ago. Our faith has changed us into different people than who we used to be. Some of the people in this park have never had a chance to hear the true message of Christianity. Please let us go back to the picnic tables and teach again. It's why God has us here."

"Not a chance," the agent said flatly. "You will stay locked up in here until you leave town. I guess God will have to find a different group of criminals to come teach us poor, ignorant people in Chicago."

"I used to be like you," Paul spoke up, addressing the agent. "I thought I was in control. I thought that I had everything at work, at home, with my money, with my whole life all set up perfectly. If anything didn't seem right, I would figure it out and fix it. If that didn't work, I would get angry and impose my will on whatever needed to be done my way. I was the king of my life. I didn't need anybody's help, and then one day God humbled me. I think He is going to humble you too. In case you haven't noticed, you're not really in charge here. You didn't decide to make Black Friday happen. You don't know what's coming or how this will end. That's why you're so scared. Your fear has you doing stupid things, trying to make you feel like you're back in control. Maybe you should consider that these men are telling the truth."

Paul's unsolicited advice wasn't helping to calm the situation insight the trailer. The longer Paul spoke, the more it appeared to be provoking Agent Anderson. Paul wasn't done upsetting the agent.

"When we got close to Chicago, Sam told me that an angry little man with a bad haircut was going to try to keep us from the work God sent us to do," Paul told Anderson. "But the little man's pride would be his downfall. I thought Sam was crazy when he said it, but here we are. I believe that God does talk to these men. Maybe He is talking to all of us, but these guys are actually listening and doing what they are supposed to do. I believe what they are saying, and you should too. They've been right about everything they've told me. More bad things are coming to Chicago. God brought them here to teach. Is that really so hard to believe? Sam also told me that the angry little man was going to die tomorrow morning before breakfast if he kept JD from teaching. It's the work God sent them here to do. I don't think it's smart to try to stop them."

Both of the soldiers standing in the trailer began to smile and look down at the floor when they heard Paul's description of the Homeland Security agent. They didn't like Anderson, and the 'angry little man' comment almost made them laugh. Paul's testimony that he believed God was speaking to JD and Sam didn't sway their opinion of the prisoners, not after hearing their arrest record. Agent Anderson was not amused.

"Are you threatening me?" Anderson asked Paul. Paul had walked up to the bars that separated them when he was speaking to Anderson. Anderson grabbed the front of Paul's shirt and pulled him up against the bars. Paul's hands were still handcuffed behind his back. Paul's nose was only a few inches from Anderson's as he yelled in Paul's face. "I can kill you right now for threatening me like that. I can shoot you and your friends for causing trouble in this camp. Martial law has been declared in this city. I AM IN CONTROL HERE! I AM GOD IN THIS TRAILER! IF YOU LIVE THROUGH THE NEXT TEN MINUTES, IT'S ONLY BECAUSE I LET YOU LIVE."

He continued to hold the front of Paul's shirt and scream at him through the bars that separated them.

"NO ONE IS GOING TO TELL ME WHO I NEED TO LET OUT OF THIS TRAILER. NO ONE IS GOING TO TELL ME HOW I SHOULD RUN THIS GODDAMN CAMP! NO ONE! DO YOU HEAR ME? NO ONE!!"

He shoved Paul against the back wall, making the trailer shake. The two soldiers standing behind the Homeland Security agent had been trading questioning looks as Agent Anderson's threats escalated. After he shoved Paul against the back wall, the female soldier took a step toward Anderson. The soldier next to her reached out a hand to stop her and shook his head no in response to her movement.

"Maybe I've taken the wrong approach," Agent Anderson said in a lower voice. He was breathing harder as his anger built. He took the Taser off his belt and pointed it toward Sam. "This packs a good punch. I had this modified. The power has been turned down so that it will NOT knock you out; it just hurts like hell as you get shocked. I bet a little pain is no big deal to somebody who's done time, right?"

He shifted the Taser, pointing it at Paul.

"I wonder if the pain would make you talk, Doc. What do you think? Do you want to change any of your answers? Is there anything you want to tell me now, or would a little juice help your memory? Do you still feel like threatening me?"

Paul stood against the back wall that Anderson had shoved him into. He didn't answer as he looked from the Taser to the cruel eyes of the agent.

"But the weakest link of this foursome might be young Luke. Maybe he can be persuaded to tell me everything you four talked about on your ride to Chicago," Agent Anderson said as he shifted the aim of the Taser toward Luke. Paul didn't say a word, but moved to stand in front of Luke. After seeing this, Sam stood in front of Paul, protecting them from the Taser

"Bad move, boys," Agent Anderson told them. "Now you're all going to feel some pain."

"Stop!"

The command came from behind Anderson. He turned slowly to face the two soldiers in the trailer. The one who had given the order to stop was a young Hispanic woman. She had her rifle up to her shoulder, ready to fire. It was aimed at his chest.

"I was ordered to guard these prisoners, sir," she told Anderson. Her voice cracked as she talked. "I...I need you to stand down, sir."

"You are making a big mistake, soldier," Agent Anderson told her. "I'm one of the good guys here. Hey, if they know something about more violence coming to this city, I need to know about it to keep people safe. That's my job. I know you think you're doing the right thing, but you don't know who you are protecting. Put that gun down. Go wait outside if you don't want to watch this."

The gun remained pointed at his chest.

"My commander told me to guard these prisoners," she said in a stronger voice. "You were going to shock that kid. You just said that he was a model student who was a good kid and hasn't been in any trouble. That's not right, sir. I can't let you do that. You need to leave now, sir," she told him.

"Are you going to shoot me?" Anderson asked her. "You look nervous. Have you ever shot anyone before? Did your training with the Illinois National Guard prepare you to kill me, or were you just playing soldier one weekend a month to pay for college?" He took a step toward her. "Maybe I should take your weapon and throw you in that cell with the rapists and murderers. That might be a real education for you. After a night with them, you'll want to shoot them, not me. But I don't want to do that. I want to find out what these prisoners know. So, if you put that gun down and walk away, I'll pretend this didn't happen."

The young woman holding the rifle glanced into the holding cell at Luke. She took the safety off of her rifle and focused her attention on Anderson again.

"You were told to leave this trailer," she told Agent Anderson. "If you take another step toward me, I will shoot you. It's time for you to leave, sir. I will be guarding these prisoners tonight."

Anderson paused, watching the young woman with the gun pointed at him, trying to read her. He didn't think she would shoot, but her hands seemed steadier, and her eyes looked more determined as she kept the rifle aimed at him. She didn't look away from him. Those dark eyes looked more dangerous than he had thought at first. *She almost looks like she wants to shoot me,* Anderson thought, as he made his decision.

"I will talk with your commander," Anderson threatened, as he walked toward the door. "I'll be back. This is not over."

"Wait!" Sam's hoarse voice stopped Agent Anderson as he opened the door to leave the trailer. The agent paused, with the door open.

"I know you are trying to do the right thing," Sam told him. "We are too. We want to go teach these people who Jesus is. We want to teach you too, but the time is short. We only have a few hours left to teach, and you only have a few hours left to make a choice. Repent, pray, and accept Jesus as your Savior. Do it now. The time is short."

The agent's face turned red with rage.

"Fuck you!" he yelled at Sam. "And fuck you too!" he yelled at the young woman who still had her rifle aimed at him. He slammed the door and was gone.

CHAPTER 20

Lynn and Padre were sitting at the airport in Kansas City, waiting to board a plane that they should have boarded hours ago. A plane had finally pulled up to their gate, but no one had been allowed to board. Several people had moved to form a line when they first saw the plane. A few angry passengers had even started chanting, "Let us on!"

A round-faced, middle-aged man was working at the ticket counter. He had been asked repeatedly, by increasingly angry passengers, when the flight was departing. He had lost his patience hours ago.

"Everyone shut up!" he yelled at the line of chanting passengers. "There are no planes going in or out of Chicago until the President and former President have landed and have been cleared from the airport. They won't give me a time for that. At some point, I will hear that you can board and take off. If you get on that plane now, you will sit on the runway going nowhere, maybe for a very long time. So, do you still want to get on the plane right now?"

The line of people that had formed grumbled as they walked back to their seats. Padre and Lynn hadn't moved. If the plane had started to board, they would have been able to move to the front of the line because of Padre's wheelchair. Padre went back to dozing in his chair. He had been up early and was exhausted. He had been worried all day about getting the wheelchair, loaded with C4, through the TSA checkpoint. He had to take his shoes and belt off, but the C4-packed wheelchair was not even checked.

Lynn went back to watching CNN on the airport TV after the excitement of the plane arriving at the gate had faded. A "Breaking News" banner was running across the bottom of the TV. She had been desensitized by the banner running across the TV every five minutes for the past two days. The banner read, "Criminals from Kansas arrested for threats of violence in Chicago." Video from Luke's phone was played. It had been cut to show JD telling the crowd at the picnic tables "believe me when I say that the violence in this city is not over." Lynn watched with increased interest. If the authorities were worried about this new threat, the security might be even tighter than expected in Chicago. It might change the schedule of the "unity event" that they were planning to sabotage. This could alter their plans.

The commentator at the national desk was talking to one of the reporters on the ground in Lincoln Park. The older man at the desk in Atlanta had a concerned scowl on his face as he talked to the young, female reporter in Chicago.

"These new threats, coming two days after the tragic deaths Friday night, are certainly concerning. Andrea, what is the response of the authorities tonight who are in the park?"

The shot on the screen shifted to Lincoln Park in Chicago. The word "LIVE" was in the lower left part of the screen. A close shot of an attractive African-American woman in her mid-thirties filled the screen. After the arrest at the picnic tables, the other reporters had gone back to the official press briefing tent. This reporter had followed the foursome under arrest. As she talked, the camera pulled back to show more of the area behind her.

"Jim, the local authorities have taken the men making these new threats into custody. They are being held in the trailer that you can see behind me. The men are being questioned right now by Homeland Security. There has been no official update other than a written statement saying that the men have violated their parole and will soon be on their way back to Kansas."

"Have these new threats changed the mood in the park tonight?" Jim asked, still using his deep, concerned voice.

Before Andrea could answer, the door to the trailer opened. Agent Anderson was outlined standing in the door. He paused, then could be heard yelling profanity back into the trailer. He slammed the door and stormed down the steps.

"Jim, we are going to see if we can get an update from the Agent who was just interviewing these men."

Andrea was moving toward Agent Anderson as she talked. She had interviewed him twice this weekend at press briefings in the tent. He had given very little new information at those briefings. She didn't think that he would give her more information than a grunt and a "no comment," but she decided to try anyway. The camera shook as her cameraman walked with her.

"Agent Anderson, Agent Anderson, can you give us an update?" Andrea yelled at the agent as she walked toward him. She had taken a path that would intercept his route back to the command center. "Have the men in custody made any new threats?"

Anderson had been ignoring her questions, walking with his head down. He had been up for over two days and was exhausted. The lines under his eyes made him look older as he turned to face the camera. He knew better than to talk to the press, but her last question struck a nerve.

"Any new threats?" he repeated to Andrea. The caption "Special Agent Anderson, Homeland Security" was now displayed on TV underneath Anderson's face.

"Yes, sir," Andrea said as she stood in front of Anderson and placed the microphone in front of his face. "Have the men in custody made any new threats, or did they offer any new details about their claim that the violence in this city is not over?"

Anderson rubbed the stubble on his face as he talked to the reporter.

"Only one new threat," the agent told her. "They told me that I would be dead by breakfast if I didn't let them out."

"They threatened to kill you?" Andrea asked incredulously.

"They told me that I would be dead by breakfast if I didn't let these criminals out of jail, so they can teach us about God. Other than that, no new threats, no new details about the threats of violence they made earlier today. But we aren't done talking to them. That's all I have for you."

With that, he turned and walked away from the short interview.

"Jim, there you have it," Andrea summed up. "These men, who have promised more violence to come, are now threatening the Homeland Security agents here. A bizarre twist to this tragedy in Chicago."

The screen shifted back to Jim at the desk in Atlanta.

"Andrea, thank you for bringing us that exclusive. When we come back, our legal team will discuss the ramifications of this new information and what that means to the effort to re-establish order in Chicago."

As the TV went to commercial, Lynn took out her phone and began searching for more information. Luke's video from the picnic tables had gone viral. She clicked the link to watch JD teach at the picnic tables. She could see that two hundred thousand people had already viewed this. This teaching was something she had never heard. She had always had a vague idea of God as an all-powerful judge. He knew if you were good or bad. You would be punished or rewarded based on what you did. This criminal, teaching about a loving, forgiving God made her feel angry and curious at the same time. She glanced at Padre. He was still sleeping. She put her earbuds back in and restarted Luke's video.

CHAPTER 21

Marco wasn't sure if he was still dreaming. He had been in and out of a restless sleep for hours. He was getting so dehydrated and weak that he couldn't resist the hands making him roll onto his back.

"I am going to turn on the light now. Close your eyes," Antonio commanded.

The light over the bed was turned on, blinding the seasick man who had not listened when he had been instructed to close his eyes.

"Hamid, you will feel a little pain when I start this IV. Hold your arm still. This might take a few tries. You are very dehydrated, and this boat keeps rocking. But you will feel much better after I get you this medicine and IV fluid. Now make a fist."

Marco held his arm still as the needle penetrated the skin. His eyes were closed because of the light. He made a fist with his left hand. The IV was placed on the second try. Antonio started a bag of IV fluid. He put a blood pressure cuff around the bag of saline, and pumped up the pressure to push the fluid in faster. After fifteen minutes the first bag of fluid had been given and Marco was feeling remarkably better. He was then given IV Zofran for nausea. A scopolamine patch was placed behind his ear and another bag of fluid was started.

As Antonio started the second liter, he spoke to the young bomb maker.

"This will make you feel better, Hamid. If you keep feeling dizzy or nauseated, I can give you more medicine. After this liter is done, you should be able to rest well. In the morning, I will make breakfast and we will get some food back into you. That will make you feel much better."

Marco lay quietly in the top bunk as Antonio continued to work on him. Antonio paused before asking the question.

"Has it ever bothered you to know that your bombs have killed and wounded so many innocent people?"

Marco hesitated. This seemed to be a trap. Why would he ask such a thing?

"I do what I am instructed to do. If the bombs are effective, that it is the will of Allah. If the bombs don't work, then that is the will of Allah. I am thankful that I can play a part in fighting the infidels who have invaded our land."

"But if your bombs kill women and children in a market, do you ever wonder if that is truly the will of Allah? Can it be His will to cause pain and suffering among innocent people?"

"I am faithful. I have been taught that it is not my will that is important, but to obey the will of Allah. To question that is sin."

"So you are willing to detonate a nuclear bomb that could kill millions of people, and if you question if this is the right thing to do, then that is a sin against God. Does that make sense to you."

"I am happy that I was deemed worthy for such an important role in the fight to defend the faith," Marco answered. "My father has watched his sons go fight for the faith. Some have died in battle, but they fought well and brought him great honor. If we are successful, I will bring more glory to my family than all of my brothers. They will sing songs of my accomplishment

I used to hate it that I was the small, near-sighted one in the family. I wanted to be a fighter with an AK-47 and hand grenades, going into battle with my older brothers. But I couldn't hit the targets when I learned to shoot, and I was so small that I wasn't good at hand-to-hand combat. Then I learned from chemistry how to make bombs. I was good at that, so they selected me to learn how to make bigger, stronger bombs. Then I was placed in a class that taught me nuclear physics. Now, I can detonate a nuclear bomb, a bomb that will bring our enemies to their knees."

Antonio didn't ask any more questions after Marco finished his answer. They waited silently for the second liter to finish being infused. Moshen took the needle out of Hamid's arm and placed a Band-Aid at the IV site.

"You called me Hamid. Are we done using other names?" Marco asked as he held his arm at the IV site.

"Yes, we don't need those names anymore. Now get some sleep, Hamid."

He turned the bright light off over the bed. He covered Hamid with a clean blanket and left the room. Hamid was suspicious. This man who had just taken care of him seemed to be a different person than the one who had punched him in the stomach two days ago. He seemed so gentle and kind, and he had asked such strange questions. It felt like a trick. Hamid didn't know what Moshen was up to, but he didn't trust him at all. He was still angry about the way he had been treated on their trip and was still looking for a way to get revenge. He fell back asleep, worried about some new twist coming from this man. He reminded himself to be very careful.

Moshen left the small bedroom and began to clean the ship's kitchen. It had been several hours since he had killed the two crew members who had been eating dinner at this table. He cleaned dried blood off the table and chairs and put the dishes in the sink. As he cleaned up, he found a Bible on a shelf next to a cookbook and a small fire extinguisher.

He sat down at the table and opened the Bible. A bookmark that was still in the Bible took him to the Gospel of John. He remembered the man on the radio talking about Chapter Three in that section of the Bible. After reading John Chapter Three several times, he read the whole Gospel of John. As he read passages about love and forgiveness, grace and mercy, his mind drifted to memories of his mother singing and rubbing his back. He could picture his grieving father, sitting at their kitchen table, staring blankly out the window. Home had become a place of quietness and grief when his mother was gone. No more singing, no more laughter.

His memories from that time in his life became filled with more time at his mosque. A young, zealous imam had seen the potential in this bright, lonely boy and had recruited him. The imam had told

Moshen that his mother would have been so proud of what he was doing, and that he would see her again in heaven.

Moshen could vividly remember the first man he had killed. This had been an important test during his training. The man was a prisoner who had been questioned by the local police. They were done with him, and now it was Moshen's job to kill him. The prisoner had been forced to dig his own grave. As he finished digging, Moshen had walked up to him, and with no warning, shot him in the head. It was similar to the killing that had happened at this table a few hours ago. The killing always left him feeling empty, and each one somehow made him feel emptier.

JD's words mixed in his brain with the childhood thoughts of family and death. He started to cry. It started quietly, but it built into big sobs that shook his body. He could see into the room where Hamid slept. He could see the two dead bodies stacked against the wall. He didn't want Hamid to hear him cry. Moshen left the galley and climbed up on deck. He was far from land at this point. Looking up, he could see countless stars. He continued to cry as the boat moved along in the darkness.

He lit a cigarette and looked up at the moon. *It can't be so simple*, he thought to himself. The sentence he heard earlier kept playing in his head. *For God so loved me, Moshen, that He gave His one and only Son, that if I believe in Him, I will have eternal life.*

CHAPTER 22

MONDAY MORNING

"Hey, wake up. Come on, big guy, rise and shine."

Sam continued to snore. He was sitting on the floor of the trailer-jail where he had fallen asleep. His head was tilted back against the wall as he slept. The big scar that ran across the front of his neck could be plainly seen.

"Hey, Prophet! Wake up!"

Sam opened his eyes to see Agent Anderson standing in front of him. The agent stuffed a piece of bacon in his mouth and chewed slowly. It was a little overcooked and crunchy. The smell of bacon made Sam's stomach growl. He glanced to his right and could see Luke lying on the floor near the back of the jail cell, still asleep. Paul was awake, sitting next to Luke. JD had been sleeping next to Sam. He woke up when Agent Anderson started talking. He yawned and stretched.

"Good morning," JD said, yawning again. "Man, I need some coffee. I was up way too late last night."

He rose and began limping around in the small cell, trying to work out the pain and stiffness.

"I slept on a bus two nights ago, and then on this floor last night. My hip is FEELING IT this morning," he said as he limped around. "I don't want to sound like I'm complaining, although I guess right now, I am complaining. I am thankful for where I am, and who God brought into my life. I am thankful that this hip was ever hurt in the first place, 'cause it led me to the truth. I am very thankful that you brought us in here last night. Your words led to a very interesting night of talking about the Word of God with my new friends. I am so glad that Paul and Luke were here to help me see what God was trying to teach me. You, yelling 'no one' at us last night like a crazy person, man, am I thankful for that. It really helped me see some of my selfish blind spots."

"Do you ever shut up?" Anderson asked him. "Seriously, can you be quiet for two minutes and let me talk?"

JD laughed out loud and looked at Sam.

"He sounds like you," JD told Sam, ignoring the request to be quiet. He turned back to Agent Anderson. "Sam is not, what you would call, a morning person. Sometimes, he'll just hold up his hand to get me to quiet down in the morning. What can I say, I wake up and I'm ready to rock 'n' roll. I'm excited to get this day going. I was down last night, but I'm back up baby," he laughed again. "I'm sorry. I don't mean any disrespect. Now let's talk about you and your relationship with God. Where are you at, in your walk with God?"

"Shut the hell up," Anderson commanded. "I came here to tell you that there has been a delay. Your ride should be here before noon. You will leave here and go back to jail for violating your parole. I'm eating breakfast, and you were wrong about me dying."

He took another bite of the crunchy bacon to emphasize his point.

JD looked at Sam and shrugged. He started to open his mouth, but closed it as Sam shook his head.

"I'm afraid you will die before WE finish eating breakfast," Sam told him. His hoarse whisper sounded worse in the morning with his dry mouth.

"Sure," Agent Anderson said sarcastically to the big man. "Well, I'm going to get some sleep while you eat breakfast. Try not to kill me. I've been up all night. We caught a couple of gang bangers who were starting fires and shooting at cops. I had a nice talk with them. What they told me makes me think that you four are a crazy annoyance, not a real threat. I don't think you know anything about what happened in this city, or what is coming. You can get some breakfast. I'm going to bed. Don't worry, I'll have someone wake me up so that I can say goodbye before you leave, unless I'm dead, of course."

Luke had woken up. He was still lying on the floor watching the interaction between Anderson and his new friends. Anderson moved to stand in front of Luke. He was tired and he was done listening to JD and Sam.

"We are still trying to reach your father," he told Luke. "You will have to stay with us until we can reach him."

Luke sat up against the back wall next to his uncle and rubbed his eyes.

"I have a question," he told Anderson. "Aren't you worried about what they just told you? Aren't you scared that you are about to die?"

Anderson let out a slow, exasperated breath. Without speaking, he turned and started to leave.

"Wait, please!" JD yelled at Anderson's back. "If you don't want to talk about your faith, let me tell you about how I came to know Christ."

Anderson didn't stop. He opened the door and left without looking back.

"Please come back!" JD yelled as Anderson left. He was standing at the bars. As the door closed, he lowered his head. Sam finally rose from the floor. He walked up to JD and put his arm around JD's shoulder.

"You tried," he said quietly to his friend. "Don't give up. There are a lot of hearts out there open to the Word."

When Agent Anderson left the small prison, he took a path behind the trailer. He had been told to stay away from the press after his interview the previous night. This route led between the hastily placed trailers and tents the Guard were using and was off limits to the press. He had his own tent with a decent cot to sleep in. He couldn't remember ever feeling so tired. He shoved the last few strips of the over-cooked bacon into his mouth just before he stepped into his tent. His first step into the tent placed his foot in a hole that had developed in the soft ground over the past two days. This caused him to fall hard against his footlocker. As he fell, he sprained his right ankle badly, and broke his right wrist against the footlocker. The bacon bits lodged in his trachea when he fell, not letting any air move past the blockage. He tried to stand up several times, but couldn't with his injured right side. He tried to yell out, but couldn't produce a sound. He hit his own stomach with his left hand as he lay on the ground, trying to perform the Heimlich maneuver. When that didn't work, he tried to roll to the tent entrance. It was difficult and painful with his injured right side. As he struggled to get back out of the tent, he became even more short of breath. He was finally able to reach out of the tent with his left arm, but everything had gone black. He lost consciousness and stopped thrashing, lying on the ground with his left arm reaching out of the tent.

CHAPTER 23

"No, you do not know what you are asking," the man speaking to them was a thin Indian man in his early thirties. He spoke very precise English with a slight accent. He was sitting in a cab at O'Hare Airport. He had been making quite a bit of money in the past two days. Reporters were landing and needing a ride into the city. The wealthy who lived in downtown Chicago were getting rides to the airport to get to any city that seemed safe. Many of the Uber drivers were scared and staying home. The taxi fares had doubled and then tripled as demand went up and competition disappeared.

Padre and Lynn had finally been able to land in Chicago. Now they were trying to get a ride to Lincoln Park. Two taxi drivers had already refused to take them to the park. Driver number three didn't look promising. Reports of snipers shooting at cars were circulating. No one was sure which rumors were true, but everyone was scared. Lynn asked how much the ride would cost, then she offered more.

“You do not understand,” the driver told her. “I will not place an attractive young woman and her disabled uncle in such a dangerous position. I do not think that you realize what you are getting into. There are stories of rape and murder in the city. The police cannot protect you. Imagine a group of young men holding a gun to your uncle’s head and making him watch while they take turns raping you. Those are some of the rumors of what is happening in the city. I will not take you there for any amount of money.”

Lynn had pushed Padre’s wheelchair up to the driver’s door. They were both facing the driver, but Lynn was doing all the talking. This was part of the plan. Her job was to manipulate the young men that they needed. She had bent down to be at eye level with the driver. This position let him look down her dress.

The driver kept looking her and Padre in the eye as they spoke. He was refusing quite a bit of money to give them a ride. He seemed to be sincerely worried about what might happen to these two strangers if he took them into the city. Lynn decided to switch tactics. She stood up straighter, and wiped away a fake tear.

“My uncle has not been able to reach his sister since Saturday morning,” she said, lying to the driver. “My aunt lives alone. Her building was burned on Friday night. She was able to call us Saturday morning, and she said that she was in Lincoln Park. We haven’t heard from her since then. She is legally blind. We are going to try to find her and take her back to Kansas City with us. We are going to go look for her, even if I have to push my uncle’s wheelchair all the way to the park. Will you please help us?”

She was standing up and had taken a step back. The driver could no longer look down her dress. He looked from Lynn to Padre, then back to Lynn.

"I will help you," he told them.

The ride was surreal. They were in Chicago, on streets that were empty except for Humvees and tanks. National Guard soldiers with M-16s were stationed at every major intersection. The radio was tuned to a local talk show. A caller was excitedly telling the host that the violence was a sign of the end of the world. The caller said that the wrath of God was coming down on the city for all the evil that had been happening in Chicago, and it would be coming soon to the rest of the country.

The driver turned down the radio and looked back at his passengers in the rearview mirror. "What do you think?" he asked them.

"I think I want to get to Lincoln Park," Padre said, trying to end the conversation.

"What about you?" The driver asked Lynn.

"I don't know," she answered. "I can't make sense of it. Violence like this seems so...so random and chaotic, and wrong, just wrong. I can't believe that this is the end of the world. This city has seen so much killing for years. The violence rips apart lives and it never seems to accomplish anything, and it never stops. I don't understand how we got to the point that we have armed soldiers in the streets. I don't know how it can ever get better."

Her voice trailed off as she stared out the window.

"My name is Raj," the taxi driver said. "At least that's the shortened version of my name that is easy to pronounce. I like reading about history. There has always been war, and killing, and chaos since the beginning of time. I am surprised that we haven't exterminated ourselves by now. When people get scared, some of them will claim that this is the end. This is certainly not the first time that people have said the world is ending. They usually want to claim that God is behind this end that they talk about. I was not born here. I have been in countries that have areas of extreme poverty, and violence, and cruelty. This country has had such a wonderful feeling of stability and security. The only thing that surprises me is that episodes like the current violence haven't happened more often here.

This country has a sense of peace and decency that has always given me hope for the future. Maybe that is changing, maybe not. "Time will tell," my father used to say.

My parents are Hindu. They believe in multiple gods. The more I learned about their religion, the less I believed in the things they taught me. I knew Muslims when I was younger. I never knew them well or tried to learn about their religion when I was younger because they were described as evil, and fights would occur between the Hindus and Muslims. When I did learn about their religion, I was struck by how many basic questions could not be answered, and how much anger I would raise by even asking simple questions.

I listened to the man called JD who spoke last night in the park. I was not in the park. I was working, but I was able to go to YouTube and watch him speak. It was extremely thought-provoking. He also has YouTube videos from when he was in prison. They show him teaching about Christianity and baptizing his fellow prisoners. I watched some of those last night too. There are rumors in the city and on the internet that he will speak again. I want to hear this man.

The idea that belief in Jesus will negate all the bad you have done does not seem fair to me. Why be a good person? How can people who have done so much wrong in this world be rewarded with heaven? In my parents' religion, your soul will keep coming back in different life forms. You will be punished or rewarded in the next life based on what you do in this life. There is a way to attain *moksha*, that is the Hindu heaven. It is by attaining self-realization and getting beyond all earthly desires. I have lived in different countries, even on different continents. I talk to dozens of different people every day. I have come to believe that we are all the same, all around this world. The same fears, and desires, and weaknesses, and greed, and lust, and pride are in us all. If the Hindus are right, no one can ever attain *moksha*. We will never get beyond our desires.

I am interested to see what this man will say today, or if they will even let him speak. I want to see if anyone can make sense of the mess that we make of this world."

They had been traveling past soldiers at checkpoints. They had been waved through the checkpoints without stopping. In this new world of violence in the streets, politically correct checkpoints had disappeared. A thin Indian taxi driver with a young woman and an older man in the back were not stopped until the last checkpoint before the park. At that checkpoint, cement barricades and a tank were backing up the soldiers who asked them to stop. They were asked why they were going to the park, then they were told that no cars were allowed beyond that point.

They parked the taxi and walked toward the park. Raj continued to insist on escorting them into the park. They were frisked before entering Lincoln Park, then they were on the road that led into camp, the same road that Paul and his new friends had been on the night before.

It was early, but the picnic tables near the cafeteria were filled with people. The only table that wasn't occupied was the table that JD had been teaching at the night before. Many of the people at the picnic tables were quietly watching the trailer that Agent Anderson had just entered with his plate of bacon. They watched expectantly as the door opened again and Anderson exited the trailer, still eating his bacon. He didn't come back for more food, but circled around behind the trailer heading toward the soldiers' sleeping quarters.

Not long after Agent Anderson walked away from the trailer, the door opened again, and the two National Guard soldiers and four prisoners exited the trailer. The crowd cheered as the four prisoners were led toward the kitchen tent for breakfast. After dishing up their trays with food, they walked to the table they had been sitting at the night before.

Sam started digging into his plate of eggs, bacon, and sausage as fast as he could chew and swallow.

"Say a quick grace and then you better throw some food down before he gets here and starts to preach," Sam said to Paul and Luke. "He can preach all morning when he gets going, and he looks ready to preach today."

They were able to sit and eat most of their food before JD made it to the table. People in the crowd had stopped him to shake his hand, hug him, and even kiss his hand or cheek. Many had tears in their eyes as they thanked him. It was being said in several languages he didn't understand.

When JD finally reached the table, he could see that D'Anthony and Leroy were back at the table next to him. The obese, older woman he had seen near them yesterday was also sitting at their table. She was singing softly to herself. Today she nodded and smiled at JD when he sat down. D'Anthony waved when he caught JD's eye. JD smiled and waved back after he put his food down.

"Are you going to kill that policeman today?" D'Anthony yelled the question from his table.

The crowd had been murmuring and pressing in closer toward JD. The large crowd became quiet, waiting to hear his answer.

"You know what I think I should do, boys?" JD asked them. He stood back up so that his booming voice could be better heard throughout the whole dining area. "I think I should pray. Will you pray with me?"

The boys nodded and folded their hands. Sam stopped chewing, bowed his head, and folded his hands. Paul, Luke, and most of the nearby crowd did the same. JD closed his eyes and looked up as he started his prayer.

"Father, thank You for this food. Thank You for the men and women who made this food and are here keeping us fed in this park. Thank You for the people in this camp and out in the city keeping us safe today. Thank You for my new friends, who reminded me last night to trust You and Your purpose, and thank You for bringing Sam into my life.

Please, Father, open blind eyes and soften the hearts of the people here today who don't know You and Your amazing love. Please give me the strength, Father, to obey You. Please use me to help bring people to the feet of Jesus. Amen"

JD unfolded his hands and looked up to the clear blue sky. He took a big breath, filling his lungs with air that was blowing in from Lake Michigan. He exhaled and brought his gaze back down to the crowd in front of him.

"Some of you may not have been here last night when I was talking," JD said in his booming, Tony Evans voice that traveled out to the edge of the crowd. "I was telling my new friends here, D'Anthony and Leroy, how I was wasting my life, getting into all kinds of trouble. I ended up in prison because I deserved to be there. I almost got killed, but my brother, Sam, stepped in and saved my life. Those men who tried to kill me stomped the hell out of my hip when they were trying to kill me. That hip has never been the same. It hurts every time I take a step, and I've been limping ever since that day. I actually love what the pain in that hip reminds me of. It reminds me of who I was before I believed in Jesus. It reminds me of who I can be when I choose to obey the God who saved me."

He limped over to Sam to lean on his shoulder.

"I don't want to bore you, but I want to tell you a little about me. I want to talk to you about how I saw the world, and how it changed when I accepted Jesus as my Savior. At the end of that, I want to ask you THE MOST IMPORTANT QUESTION that you will EVER be asked. So, please stick around for that."

He would turn from side to side as he talked, trying to look at all of the people who were gathered there listening. He would stumble and wince when he turned to his right.

"Brother, I need help again," he said quietly to Sam. Sam nodded and rose from the picnic table. He picked his friend up again and placed JD on his shoulders like a small child. JD gave him a thank-you pat on the shoulder and went back to speaking to the crowd. Sam looked down at the ground and prayed for his friend.

"When I was in prison, they used to make me talk to a shrink, twice a month, whether I wanted to or not. He helped me realize that I had this tribal view of the world. That meant that I cared about a small group of people, my 'tribe,' but I didn't give a damn about anybody else. I think a lot of us see the world that way. When I was little, my tribe was me, and my mom, and my little brother, and a few friends. When I got older, the gang I was in became my tribe. It was strange how much I hated everybody who was not in my tribe. I didn't care about anybody or anything except for the circle of people that I thought was family. I thought they would always have my back.

Then one day, I'm getting beaten and I think I'm going to die, and the only person who comes to help me is this big, goofy looking, white boy. He saved my life, but then he took care of me when I was so hurt I couldn't take care of myself. It may be the only time I remember somebody being really kind to me. But he wasn't just good to me, he took care of everybody. It didn't matter if you were white, or black, or Hispanic, or even what you did to get you put in prison. He was just there to take care of you if you needed help. Living like that put him at risk in prison, but he still did it.

While I was laying there, bored and in pain in the infirmary, I started listening to some good Bible teachers. I didn't want to listen to them, but that's what the guard in the infirmary had on his radio every morning. At first, I couldn't stand to hear Bible teaching. But pretty soon, I was looking forward to it every day. I started learning, and praying, and I accepted Jesus as my personal Savior. As I learned more, I even started teaching other inmates about the grace and peace of God.

A few weeks ago, Sam told me that violence and chaos were coming to Chicago, and that God wanted me to go preach there. At first, I didn't believe him. I didn't think the horrible violence of Friday night would happen, and I couldn't believe that God would want ME here teaching. There's just got to be somebody better for the job, right?

But I realized that Sam was telling me the truth, and that God did want us here. But even when I showed up here last night, I had this broken part of me that still saw the world in this crazy tribal way. The new group I saw as 'my tribe' were the criminals and the kids in gangs that had been turning away from the Lord their whole lives. I wanted them to see the truth, but this broken part of me didn't really care about the good people in this park who had been trying to live right. It was my own bias keeping me from seeing the world the way God wanted me to see it. There are a lot of people in this park who have not done stuff that would get them sent to prison. They are decent people, trying to do their best each day. Those people were not part of MY PLAN of who I was trying to reach when I got here to Chicago.

So God put some wonderful people in my life to remind me of what His Word says about HIS plan. I want to thank You, Father, for my new friends and what they reminded me of last night. I want to especially thank Agent Anderson."

He paused and took a drink that Sam handed him. He looked around at the large crowd that was listening, then continued.

"What Agent Anderson said to us last night, I guess he actually yelled it at us last night, reminded me of some of the most amazing parts of the Bible. I had the words 'No One' bouncing around in my head after he left us last night. I told Paul and Luke about that. They reminded me of what the apostle Paul wrote to the believers in Rome a long time ago. He wrote this:

'There is no one righteous, not even one; there is no one who understands; there is no one who seeks God. All have turned away, they have together become worthless; there is no one who does good, not even one.'

JD paused to let his words sink in. The crowd had grown while he spoke. Some people near the back of the crowd pushed closer. The TV cameras in the park were focused on him and the crowd around him. He took another drink, then he was back to teaching.

"The apostle Paul keeps going; he says that NO ONE is declared righteous in God's sight by the works they do. For ALL have sinned and have fallen short of the glory of God.

Here's where I messed it up in my brain. I wanted to think only about this amazing, forgiving God who would forgive people, like me, who have done a lot of bad things. Like I said, that was who I saw as my new tribe: criminals who were ready to turn their lives around. I wasn't thinking about everyone else. I know that was a messed up way to think, but it was still how I saw the world. There were bad people who needed to hear His Word and receive His forgiveness, and I was coming here to reach them. And there were good people who probably really didn't need to hear me preach, but it was okay if they listened anyway. That was my very wrong perspective on who I was here to reach.

But God reminded me of HIS WORD. He reminded me that we are all in one big tribe of people called sinners. WE ALL disobey God in some way, and WE ALL need the forgiveness that comes through believing in His Son.

That leads me to asking you the most important question you will ever be asked. Are you ready for this?

WHO IS JESUS CHRIST?" He paused and looked around at the crowd, trying to look into as many eyes as he could.

"That's it. Who is Jesus Christ?" he paused again.

"Jesus even asked His own disciples this question. At first, He asked them 'who do people say I am,' then He asked 'who do you say I am?' While you think about that, I'm going to tell you who Jesus said He was. He told His disciples, the night before they crucified Him, 'I am the way, and the truth, and the life.' He said, 'NO ONE comes to the Father EXCEPT THROUGH ME.' That means that the ONLY way to God, to heaven, to forgiveness of your sins, is by believing that Jesus died as a sacrifice for your sins, so that you can be united with the God who loves you. United in heaven one day when you die, and united in spirit with Him while you are still on this earth, the second you believe.

Last night, I was reminded of one more part in the Bible where the words 'No One' were used. Jesus is teaching Nicodemus. And He tells Nick, 'NO ONE can see the kingdom of God unless he is born again.' Nicodemus didn't understand that when Jesus was talking to him. I wouldn't have gotten it either at first. He was talking about a spiritual rebirth. He was talking about the choice you make of who you believe in, and how you answer that question. When I figured out how to answer THE MOST IMPORTANT QUESTION, I knew it was time to say this prayer. You can pray it with me right now if God has opened your heart. Here goes."

JD folded his hands and closed his eyes.

"Father, I know I'm a sinner, a sinner who is separated from You because of my disobedience. I know I cannot pay for my sins by the things I do, but they can be taken away and made clean by WHO I believe in. I know that You love me so much that You sent Your son, Jesus, to suffer and die as punishment for MY sins. You raised Him up, showing that death has no power over Him. He is MY personal Savior, and the Savior for all the people here who believe in Him. Thank You for loving me and opening my eyes, Father. Amen."

JD paused, as many in the crowd murmured, 'Amen.'

"Time for very good news!" he said, as he looked back down at the crowd. "The apostle Paul wrote to the early church, that if you believe in your heart that Jesus is Lord, and profess that with your mouth, then you are saved! If you just prayed that prayer with me, if you believe in your heart that Jesus is your Savior, YOU HAVE JUST BECOME A CHILD OF GOD!! WELCOME TO THE FAMILY, BABY!!"

Most of the people at the picnic tables were clapping and cheering. A few had angrily walked away as JD spoke. The people who could reach JD were hugging his legs and crying. Sam was in the middle of a crushing group of celebrating new believers. The loudspeaker broke in, interrupting the celebration.

"Medics are needed at the command center now! Medics to the command center now!"

The group at the tables became quiet as they watched National Guard soldiers run toward the command center. An ambulance pulled up the road, stopping at the tents that were difficult to see from the picnic tables. The loudspeaker broke in again.

"Leave the picnic tables when you have finished eating."

It was repeated in Spanish.

Despite the announcement, no one left the picnic tables. The reporters, who had been filming JD and the scene at the tables, were scrambling to get as close as they could to the new action near the command center. They were kept at a distance by soldiers as Agent Anderson was taken from his tent and loaded into an ambulance. Chest compressions were being performed as the ambulance left the park. After the ambulance pulled away, the small cluster of National Guard soldiers turned to face JD. Some of the soldiers took a few steps toward the picnic table. M-16s were out, pointing at the ground. They were tired and scared. The fear was now turning into anger. The anger had been loosely focused on criminals they could not see, sniping from the shadows at friends. Now the anger had a focus. It was focused on the man who told Agent Anderson that he would die today. They were blaming JD for his death. The order hadn't been given yet, but the soldiers were prepared to take this man back into custody and put him back in the mobile jail. If he resisted, they were willing to use whatever force it took to get the job done. The crowd at the picnic tables saw this, and moved in front of JD to protect him.

Sam hit JD's leg three times to get his attention. He folded his hands and held them up for JD to see.

"I want everyone who can hear me to fold your hands!" JD's loud, preaching voice had been turned up a notch. "You heard me, fold your hands! Kneel down if you have room to kneel. Come on now, do it! It is time to pray!" JD yelled loud enough for everyone to hear him. "It is time to reach out to our loving Father."

Paul and Luke knelt down by their picnic table. The media had turned their cameras back to the action at the tables. They filmed as more people near the picnic tables knelt down. A few of the National Guard soldiers removed their helmets as JD began to pray.

"Father, I don't understand all of this. There has been so much pain and grief this weekend as we watch people we know and care about getting hurt and getting killed. Please, Father, use all of this fear and pain and ugliness to help open our hearts to You and to how much we need You in our lives. Help us grow closer to You. Please let all the people here feel your peace and love. Please let Agent Anderson and his family and friends feel the comfort and love that can only come from You. Thank you for bringing us here today. Thank You for opening our eyes to You, Lord. Amen."

Sam unfolded his hands and flashed JD a thumbs-up to show his approval. The people listening murmured, 'amen,' as they unfolded their hands and rose to their feet. Sam patted JD on the leg three times to get his attention again. When JD looked down at him, Sam pointed toward Lake Michigan.

"The announcement said to clear out away from these tables," JD told the crowd. "So we are going to head down to the lake. I want to tell you about two of my favorite chapters in the Bible. God gave us a beautiful day. Let's go down by the water and talk about the God who loves you. This is going to be great! Follow me, everybody."

Paul and Luke stood up, ready to follow JD and Sam to the lake. Sam tapped Paul on the shoulder and pointed at JD's uneaten breakfast. He motioned for Paul to hand him the plate. Paul could see Sam's lips moving, but couldn't hear him as he asked for the plate of food. Paul understood the hand gesture. He took JD's plate off the table and handed it up to him. As he did, Sam leaned in close enough to be heard.

"You and Luke need to head back to your car. Don't follow us to the lake," Sam instructed him. "Go west, away from the city. Get away as fast as you can; run when you're out of the park. When you get to Iowa, get off the main roads. God has other plans for you my friend. Go see your father before he dies. You don't have much time."

Sam placed a big hand on Paul's shoulder and squeezed gently to say goodbye. He turned to Luke, briefly placed his hand on Luke's head, then winked at him. Then he turned away from the tables and began to walk slowly toward the lake, parting the sea of people who kept crying and thanking JD. As Sam walked away, he began singing in his hoarse voice.

Paul could see Sam's lips moving as he sang, but he couldn't hear Sam's raspy voice above the crowd. A wall of humanity was following JD and Sam to the lake, and they now blocked Sam from Paul's sight. He could still see JD, high above the crowd. The soldiers, who were still present at the picnic tables, looked for direction from the corporal on-site. He was the one who had taken the foursome into custody the previous night. This morning, he was a changed man. He had prayed with JD, and he was now a child of God.

"Let them go," the corporal commanded as he placed the helmet back on his head. "Secure this area and await further orders."

Paul turned away, having seen his new friends for the last time. He and Luke walked toward the kitchen as the crowd drifted toward the lake. They held empty plates and appeared to be going back for seconds on eggs and sausage. All eyes were focused on the group walking toward Lake Michigan. The reporters and their camera crews were trailing behind the crowd. Instead of getting more food, Paul led Luke around the back of the food service tent, away from the crowd and the picnic tables. They kept walking and were soon out of the park and moving through Chicago streets that were still full of debris and the smell of fire. As soon as they were out of the park, they began to run.

CHAPTER 24

"Are you crying?" Padre asked incredulously.

He had rotated his wheelchair so he could see Lynn. She had been standing behind him listening to JD. She had covered her face with her hands and was quietly crying.

"Jesus, Lynn," Padre said with disgust. "What the hell is wrong with you?"

Raj took out a tissue from his back pocket and blew his nose. He had tears in his eyes as well. He wiped them away as he talked.

"I'm sorry," he told Lynn. "I only have this one Kleenex, and my nose was starting to run." He blew his nose again and put it back in his pocket. "That was very touching," Raj said, gesturing toward JD and the group walking toward the lake. "I have had many discussions about religion with my father and my brother. My father holds on to the Hindu traditions that he learned from his parents. My younger brother is now an atheist. I tell them both that what they believe does not make sense to me. This amazingly complex world did not come about by chance. Many in my family were doctors. I would read some of their textbooks out of curiosity. The human body is an amazing miracle. Random chance did not bring together billions of cells to run the most complex organism in the world. The atheists do not have even the beginning of a rational argument for how to explain life. The only logical explanation is that a superior, intelligent being, God if you will, is the ultimate creator. If you then believe that there is a god, or gods, then you have to wonder which one is real. There are so many religions, so many different beliefs, so how do you know which one is right? I have read about many of these religions. Many people think that they are all similar, with only minor differences. The truth is that they have only superficial similarities and major differences. The core beliefs and exclusivity of their doctrines are vastly different.

This man makes an amazingly simple, but strong, argument for belief in Jesus. I feel so moved when I listen to him. To believe that there is a God who is ready to love and forgive you for all of your sins, and all you have to do is believe that Jesus paid the price for your sins, it almost seems too easy. I have been taught for so long that you must personally pay for what you have done wrong. That is what seems fair to me. But he lays out so plainly that we all disobey God and cannot earn His forgiveness with our actions. It is an intriguing idea.

The idea of a loving God who would send His Son as a sacrifice to pay the price for our sins, that idea is different from all the other religions that tell you to earn your forgiveness with good works. I love the way he put together the need for God making this sacrifice by saying that no one is worthy, no one lives a sinless life, NO ONE is able to live the life that is completely able to obey God with every thought and every urge and every action. How did this criminal receive such teaching? How did he come here, with no formal training, and teach with such knowledge and eloquence? He is a gifted speaker. I must go to the beach and hear what else he has to say. I can help you get down to the beach," he offered to Padre

"He does bring up some very interesting points," Padre told the taxi driver, trying to sound genuine. "But I really want to look through the campsite for my sister. I didn't see her in the group that was going down to the lake."

Raj looked questioningly at Lynn. She looked down at Padre.

"I'll stay and help look for my aunt," she said, "Goodbye, Raj. Thank you very much for the ride today."

She stepped toward him and gave him a quick hug, making him smile. Padre surprised him by facing him and opening his arms.

"Can I give you a hug too?" he asked Raj. Padre sniffled loudly and pretended to wipe nonexistent tears from his eyes. "It's been quite a weekend, and you are the kindest person we have met on this strange trip."

"Of course," the taxi driver said. He bent down low to awkwardly hug Padre in his wheel chair. Padre held him tight, finishing the hug with a big pat on the man's back. As he did this, he slipped the keys to the taxi out of Raj's coat pocket. Padre wiped away more fake tears with his right hand after the hug. With his left hand he hid the car keys under his leg.

"Good luck. I hope you find your sister," Raj told Padre as he straightened up. "I hope to see you both again soon," he said, looking from Padre to Lynn. Then he turned and started walking after the ten-foot-tall Chris Rock look-alike who was moving toward Lake Michigan.

As soon as he was out of sight, Padre turned and started moving away from the park.

"We got lucky that he walked down to the beach. We need his car to get to the Cathedral on time. I was almost ready to switch to plan B." Padre told Lynn as he started wheeling away from the park.

Lynn knew that plan A was to get close and detonate the bomb as the political big shots were going into the cathedral. If that wasn't possible, Plan B was to get them after the service as they came out of the church. They both knew that the sooner they could detonate the bomb, the better their chance of success. They didn't want to spend more time than necessary near a small army of Secret Service agents in a wheelchair loaded with explosives.

Lynn was quiet as she followed Padre out of the park. She looked back over her shoulder at the group walking toward the water. She wished that she had gone with Raj to the beach, but she was loyal to Padre. She had growing doubts about executing this plan. She had been touched by listening to JD. The phrase that she heard last night continued to play in her head. Once again, she put her name in the sentence that she had never heard before listening to JD.

For God so loved me, Lynn Mendez, that He gave His one and only Son as a sacrifice for my sins, so I could be forgiven. For God so LOVES ME, she thought. Raj was right. It hadn't seemed fair that God would forgive horrible people, but now it made sense. Religion had always seemed like a waste of time, but the message of love and forgiveness kept calling to her. She could never remember a message of love in her life. She had been raised by an unstable mother who had a series of rotating boyfriends that she had lived with. Her mother had been abusive, and some of the boyfriends had been abusive. Lynn had two half-sisters and one half-brother that she had no contact with. They all had different fathers. Padre had been the closest thing to a stable family, and a decent father figure, that she had ever known. She had been so alone and scared before she met him. She still felt alone much of the time, but now she felt more in control.

The thought that someone could know all of the bad things she had done and would still love her, even die for her, left her quiet and confused. JD's voice ran through her brain again as she walked back to the taxi with Padre. *For God so loves Lynn Mendez that He gave His one and only Son, that if I believe in Him, I will be forgiven of all my sins and have eternal life. Could that really be right?* she wondered as she helped Padre get into the taxi. The growing feeling of excitement in her heart told her that it was.

CHAPTER 25

The ship's galley was a cramped area. Hamid was sitting at the table while Moshen finished cooking. Hamid was no longer seasick. The medicine and IV fluids had worked beautifully. The smell of the cooking food was making his stomach growl. They had been listening to the short-wave radio again. Moshen had brought it from the bedroom to the small kitchen. Hamid was not happy with the teaching that they were hearing on the radio. It was blasphemy. This man would have been arrested and executed if he had spread these lies in Hamid's country. It made him more eager to drive this ship into the infidel city and detonate the nuclear bomb. Someone needed to stop this blasphemy before it deceived more people.

When Hamid protested, Moshen told him to be quiet and let him hear what this man had to say. Hamid quieted down as Moshen placed eggs, coffee, juice, and toast on the table in front of him. Hamid was famished and focused on the food in front of him. Moshen was quiet as he served breakfast and listened to the radio. At times, he would walk closer to the radio to hear it better. He even appeared to tear up when JD finished praying at the picnic tables. There was a pause in the teaching as JD started walking toward Lake Michigan.

Moshen turned the radio down and refilled his coffee cup. He dished some of the eggs onto his own plate and sat down across from Hamid.

"What do you think about this man's teaching?" he asked Hamid.

Hamid was startled by such a question. "He should be killed," he said angrily. "This is blasphemy. It is clear what the Koran says about such men. My father..."

He was interrupted by Moshen.

"I know what the Koran says, and I know what the imams teach, but what do you believe?"

Hamid paused before answering. He was still worried that this man was trying to trick him.

"I believe," he said slowly, "that it is a sin not to obey the words of the Prophet."

"You know that the Koran teaches that Jesus was a prophet. He is supposed to return at the end of the world to serve the Twelfth Mahdi and to help lead nonbelievers back to Islam," Moshen said

"I know what the Koran says about this," Hamid answered.

"I don't understand how He can be a prophet, and yet we are not supposed to believe His own teaching. I have been listening to this man teach in Chicago. You have been listening, and understanding the man. You hear him in Farsi. I hear him speaking Italian, some English, and a little Farsi. How is this possible? Could it be that God is trying to get our attention, that He wants us to hear the truth and to believe? Do you have any other explanation for something so incredible happening?"

Hamid rose from the table and carried his plate and glass to the sink. "I will not listen to this!" he yelled at his companion.

Moshen sat at the table, looking down at his plate as he continued.

"This morning, while I served you breakfast, I said the prayer," Moshen said, tearing up. "I told God that I am a sinner, separated from Him by my sin. I told Him that I believed that He sent Jesus to die to pay for my sins, so that I could be forgiven and have eternal life. He did this because He loves me. That is so hard for me to believe, but I know it's true. I am now a child of God, and it feels so good. I feel at peace, maybe for the first time in my life."

Hamid stood at the sink, feeling his anger build. He dropped the plate in the sink and grabbed the top of the fire extinguisher in front of him on the shelf. Moshen had his back to the sink. He didn't see Hamid as he swung the extinguisher.

"Enough!" Hamid yelled, as the extinguisher struck Moshen's right temple. Moshen lost consciousness as the blow knocked him onto the floor. Hamid continued to grip the top of the extinguisher. He took more big swings with the extinguisher, connecting several times with Moshen's ribs, arms, and face as he lay helplessly on the floor.

"That is enough! Enough! Enough from you!" Hamid screamed at Moshen's unconscious body as the blows rained down.

The top of the extinguisher broke off, spewing white powder all over the small kitchen. Hamid threw the top of the extinguisher at Moshen's unconscious body. He kicked the cabinets in the small kitchen and flipped the small table onto its side.

"I knew I would kill you!" he yelled at Moshen's unconscious body. "You should not have hit me, or treated me like a child. Now look at you. Did your false god protect you? NO! Allah has delivered you into my hands. And now, I will detonate a nuclear bomb and destroy one of the infidel's cities. I will show the world that their false teaching cannot stand against the will of Allah."

Hamid wiped the blood and white powder on his hands onto the sides of his pants and walked into the bedroom to arm the bomb. *This will be a great day*, he thought to himself. *I will be one of the greatest martyrs in history. They will write songs of what I did to the enemies of the faith. My whole village will kneel down before my family to honor me after this day.*

CHAPTER 26

Lynn was driving from Lincoln Park to the downtown cathedral. Padre was sitting next to her in the front passenger seat of Raj's stolen taxi. She was listening to the radio broadcasting live from Lincoln Park as she drove. They had to move slowly through the streets due to abandoned cars and National Guard checkpoints. There had been a pause in JD's teaching as he moved from the picnic tables to the edge of Lake Michigan. Now his voice was back on the radio. She was happy to crawl slowly through the streets of Chicago and listen to JD teach. Padre was not nearly as patient.

"Now I want to tell you about two of my favorite parts of the Bible," JD said as he surveyed the growing crowd on the beach. He was still sitting on top of Sam's broad shoulders. "The reason I love these parts of the Bible is that they apply to everyone who can hear my voice. That's right, if you can hear my voice, this is about you."

Lynn turned up the radio's volume. Padre gave her an annoyed look but didn't turn it back down. The reporters in Lincoln Park had trailed the crowd down to the beach, sensing that JD and Sam were better for ratings than dry updates from the National Guard commander on-site. JD's booming voice was easily picked up by the network microphones.

"Y'all can sit down if you want," JD told the crowd. "Get comfortable, I can preach a long time when I get going."

JD paused to let the crowd settle in. No one sat down. The back of the crowd continued to fill in with stragglers. The large woman who had been sitting at the picnic table with D'Anthony and Leroy was standing right beside the boys. Her name was Estella. JD didn't know her name; in his mind, he had nicknamed her Mama Bear. The first time he had talked to the boys at the picnic tables, he had seen her moving closer to the boys while she gave JD her angry mom look. Her maternal, protective instincts had kicked in when she saw that the boys were alone in the park. She was tough and had chased a few people away from the boys who didn't look right to her. She wasn't sure about JD when he first sat down near the boys. She was glad now that she hadn't chased him away.

D'Anthony was holding her hand. Leroy knew that he was too old to hold hands, but he felt better that she was there with them. The police were reassuring, but they weren't always around. Leroy realized that this woman was always watching out for them. Estella was happy to do it. These boys reminded her of her own boys when they were young. She had been humming softly as she walked down to the beach. Beautiful, old songs that she had learned in church when she was a child, had been playing in her head. She stopped humming to herself as JD paused.

"Let's get this started," she yelled at JD, sparking laughter and applause from the crowd around her.

"Yes, ma'am," JD said, smiling. "Here we go." He projected his naturally loud voice well enough to be heard at the back of the crowd.

"The part of the Bible I want to talk about this morning is in Luke, Chapter 15. I want to talk about a story Jesus told about two brothers and their father. Like I said, this applies to everyone in the world, that's right, EVERYONE! When Jesus is teaching, there are several times that He tells people that you are one of two groups: you are a sheep or a goat, you are on the narrow road or the wide road, you are the wheat or the chaff, and in this story, you are either the older brother or the younger brother. All these stories say the same thing: basically, you are in one of two groups in God's eyes, saved or unsaved. And which one of those groups you are in goes back to how you answer the most important question, like we talked about earlier.

Now, it's important to understand who Jesus is talking to when He tells this story. I think that this story was directed at the self-righteous, religious leaders who hated Jesus. The Jewish leaders of that day thought that people belonged in two groups. The first group were those who became righteous by following all the crazy rules they told people they had to follow. The religious leaders taught that those rules came from God, and that following those rules made you better in the eyes of God. Now, before you get upset with me, I know that God gave people rules to live by; He still does. He gave the Ten Commandments. But He did this to show these people that they WERE NOT righteous in God's sight because they kept breaking His Commandments. You don't know you're speeding until you see a sign that tells you the speed limit. You don't know you are a sinner unless God gives you a set of His rules, and you realize that you keep breaking the rules.

These religious leaders took those Ten simple Commandments and made a bunch more rules. Most of these man-made rules were ridiculous, like how many steps you could take on the Sabbath. I'm not kidding. They actually thought that if you took too many steps on Saturday, then you just sinned against God. So the second group of people, as the Jewish leaders saw it, were the sinners, the ones who didn't follow all these rules, or they didn't follow them well enough.

Well, Jesus has been hanging out with group number two, the sinners. The Jewish religious leaders would have never spent time with these people. Those leaders knew that they were better than this group of 'sinners.' Following all those rules gave them a sense of being righteous in their own eyes. Jesus has been rocking their world, and He's about to do it again with this story.

So there are two brothers in this story. The younger one is a rude, defiant son. He comes to his father and wants his inheritance. Basically, he tells his dad, 'I wish you were dead.' That's when he would have normally gotten the inheritance, when his father was dead. At that time, they are living in a culture where honor is very important. In that culture, the father should have slapped that kid and maybe kicked him out of the house. You've got to teach that boy a lesson, his friends would have told him.

Instead, what the father does is to give the boy the money he would get for his inheritance, and then the boy leaves. He is off to the big city to party. He spends all his money living it up. Then the money is gone, his friends are gone, and the party's over. Then comes a famine in the land and this kid can't find work. He ends up feeding pigs and wishing he had as much food to eat as those pigs.

It is hard for us to imagine how bad that sounded to the people listening to that story. A good Jewish boy was not supposed to touch pork. Not cook it, not eat it, and definitely not hang out feeding the pigs. This boy has gotten as low as a good Jewish boy can get. He is on this farm, without enough food to eat and he realizes that he should go back to his father. He knows he doesn't deserve to be treated like part of the family anymore; he has screwed up way too bad for that. His plan is to beg his father to let him stay on as a hired hand. So, the boy starts heading home.

The boy's father has been watching for him, hoping to see him come home. Before the boy gets to his village, his father sees him and runs to meet him. Now in that culture, men didn't run. It was a shameful act to show your skinny, old legs. Today, people put on silly looking running outfits and go running in public all the time. At that time, it would have embarrassed the heck out of this man to be seen running in public. But he does it anyway because he's so excited to see his son.

So, the father runs up to his son. The boy starts to apologize, but before he can finish his apology, his father is kissing him and hugging him. He puts the family ring back on his son's finger, letting his son know that he is back in the family, and then he puts a fancy robe on this dirty, stinky kid.

In this story, the father represents God. He is a loving, forgiving father. When the boy has repented, the father is ready to welcome him back into the family. The father knows this boy's heart, and he is ready to forgive him, because his child is truly sorry for what he has done.

Jesus is trying to teach these people that God is ready to forgive those who have disobeyed Him if they are ready to turn back to Him. The way you turn back to God and get good with Him, is to admit that you are a sinner, separated from him by the disobedience in your life. When you accept Jesus Christ as your personal savior, meaning that you believe He died as punishment for your sins, you are forgiven. That's when you have become a part of God's family. You have been spiritually born again. Isn't that beautiful?

You are NOT going to get good with God by thinking you are doing everything right and you don't need His forgiveness. The people who think that way are self-righteous fools. They are NOT born again as children of God and they WILL NOT enter His kingdom.

I used to see myself as the younger brother in the story. I didn't deserve to ever be forgiven. I had lived my life as far away from obeying God as I could. I used to have trouble believing that God would want me back in the family. This story, about how forgiving and loving God is, is one of my favorites. It says earlier in this chapter that when a sinner turns back to God, there is a party in heaven. It says that the angels in the presence of God celebrate when just one sinner, JUST ONE, repents and accepts Jesus as their personal Savior."

JD paused as yells of 'Amen' came from the crowd on the beach.

"I sure hope," JD continued. "Those angels, in the presence of God, are getting worn out this weekend from all the partying they've been doing!"

Cheering and louder yells of 'Amen' came from the crowd on the beach. Lynn could clearly hear the yells from the crowd coming through on her radio. She had found an open parking garage near the church where the former President was scheduled to speak. Security was tight, but not as tight as it was a few miles away at the church the current President would be speaking at later today. She pulled into a spot, but kept the car running and the radio on. Padre changed into his old police uniform as she listened to JD teach. Part of the plan to get close to the former President, would be to use his old uniform. He thought that being a retired cop in a wheelchair would get him special treatment, and make him seem less threatening to the security team around the former President.

On the beach by Lake Michigan, JD paused to wipe his nose and the tears from his eyes. He raised his hands to quiet the crowd. His strong voice could be heard up and down the beach, and clearly on the radio in the stolen taxi.

"But this story is not over. Remember, this father has two sons. Jesus is talking to the Pharisees, the religious leaders of the time, and He has been building this story to bring it back to them and the horrible attitude that they have toward 'sinners.' Jesus is about to show these leaders that they were actually the ones breaking the rules that God thinks are important.

The older brother has been out in the field. There is a party going on at his father's house. By the way, the Father's house is what Jesus is using to represent heaven. So the younger brother has been gone. He is back, and there is a big, blowout party. This is a big deal. The older brother should have been there. He should have been told about his brother coming home, and he should have come running to welcome him back. He should have been helping to get that party started. But his father did not tell him about his younger brother coming home, and he was not told for a very good reason.

The father knows what's in this son's heart.

The older brother has a bitter, jealous, unforgiving, unloving heart. This boy is not going to come and celebrate that his brother is home. He is mad that his brother is being forgiven and welcomed back home. HE DOES NOT LOVE HIS BROTHER! HE DOES NOT FORGIVE HIM! He doesn't even love his own father. This son has been playing by the rules that he thinks are important. He gets up and works each day. He does it with a bad attitude, but he thinks that's all he needs to do to be a good person and please God. He thinks that if he follows the rules that he thinks are important, even if he doesn't show love or kindness to his family, then he is doing okay. That's what these religious leaders are doing too. They have a few rules they want to follow, even though they have no love or compassion in their hearts. In John Chapter Eight, it talks about them finding a young girl committing adultery. They bring her to Jesus, trying to trap Him. They say to Jesus that the law says we are supposed to kill her. They want Jesus to choose if they should kill her or not. They think they can trap Jesus if He gives the wrong answer. They think that the right answer is to NOT forgive her, to NOT be merciful, but to kill her.

But Jesus is rocking their world with ideas very different from what they have always believed. Jesus has told them that loving each other is now one of the big rules He wants people to follow. The night before they crucified the Lord, Jesus told His disciples, 'My command is this: love each other.'

If you go back and read the Sermon on the Mount in Matthew, Jesus is teaching people that God sees your heart. If you look at a woman lustfully, then you have committed adultery with her in your heart. Those lustful thoughts are sins the way God sees them. You may not think that's a big deal, but God says that looking at a woman that way, and having those thoughts in your heart, means that you're disobeying Him.

Jesus also teaches that if you remain angry toward your brother or sister, that is sin. You are disobeying God with that attitude. That older brother had a horrible, unloving, unforgiving attitude toward his brother and his father. His attitude was keeping him out of the party in his father's house, meaning his sin is keeping him out of heaven. Now, everybody's sin keeps them out of heaven, but the younger brother knew that he had messed up badly and needed his father's forgiveness. The older boy thought that he was doing good enough and didn't need to be forgiven.

The story ends right there. That boy is faced with a choice, just like everyone who is listening to me. He can change his heart, ask for his father's forgiveness, and start to love these wonderful people God put in his life, or he can stay an angry, unloving, unforgiving person, and never get into that party in his father's house. If he changes his heart, he will no longer see himself as the 'good' kid. If he starts seeing himself the way God sees him, he will see all the ugly sin in his own heart. He will realize that he is no better than that younger brother. He will ask for his Father's forgiveness. If you are realizing today, that you are that older brother and you need God's forgiveness, His forgiveness comes by realizing that Jesus died for you, so that all that awful sin can be completely forgiven.

You may still have trouble realizing who you are. Maybe anger and lust aren't your sins. Maybe your heart is full of pride. God hates that one too. Or maybe jealousy, coveting, anxiety, not trusting the Lord, or greed is what fills your heart and your thoughts. God sees all of that. He knows who you really are, what's really in your heart, and He is ready to forgive you. Why? Because He loves you. He is waiting for you to turn back to Him and be forgiven. Those angels, who live in the presence of God, are ready to keep partying over another lost sheep who is found."

JD paused and surveyed the crowd. The crowd had grown quiet. Many were looking down at the sand with folded hands. Some were quietly weeping. The 'amens' were much more subdued.

"That is a lot to take in," he said in a quieter voice. "There is some mind-blowing, life-changing truth in what you just heard. I hope that God is opening your heart to the truth. I pray that He is opening the eyes of spiritually blind people right now. Hearing all this may make you defensive and angry, or maybe make you feel very confused. It might be different than beliefs you have held your whole life, even if you've been sitting in church every Sunday morning. You may need some time to sort this out. I want you to have time to talk to the God who loves you, and to answer THE BIG QUESTION. But I want to talk for just a few more minutes before I finish up. I want to finish up by talking about one of my very favorite passages in the Bible. This is in Luke, Chapter 23."

JD paused, taking in a big breath of fresh air that tasted like Lake Michigan. He liked that smell. He was glad that his last day would be here, on a beach with Sam, with the smell of the lake. He glanced down at D'Anthony and Leroy. *Please open the hearts of these boys*, he quietly prayed. He scanned the large crowd that had followed him down to the lake. *Please, Father, open all their eyes*, he prayed.

Sam patted his leg again. It was a signal to get back to preaching. Sam had reminded him again on the way to the beach that their time was running short. *What would I have ever done without Sam?* he asked himself. *Thank You, Father for putting Sam in my life*, he prayed before he resumed his talk on the beach. Sam was staring down at the sand with tears running down his face. His lips moved as he quietly prayed for his friend. And then the big, booming voice was again coming from the little man on his shoulders.

"This is one of my favorite parts of the Bible. It might be because I've been a criminal for pretty much my whole life. There are times I've had my doubts about whether God would really love me and want me, 'cause He knows all the bad stuff I did. He even knows about the stuff I thought about doing and wanted to do. That's overwhelming for me to think about. I know I don't deserve to be forgiven for all that. I haven't done anything good enough to earn all that love and forgiveness, but God is giving it to me anyway. The grace and mercy of our loving God is the most beautiful thing in the world.

So, in the 23rd Chapter of Luke, Jesus is being crucified. He is actually nailed to that wooden cross and is dying. There are two other criminals with Him being crucified that day, one on His left, one on His right. I think that God is again showing everyone in the world that you are in one of two groups. You are either the criminal on the left, or the one on the right.

One of the criminals is hanging there, dying, and he is insulting Jesus as he dies. He is actually taunting Jesus as they are all hanging on their own crosses. He yells at him, 'hey buddy, I thought you were supposed to be the Messiah. If you can, why don't you work one more of those miracles and get us all down from here?'

The other criminal hanging there yells at the guy who is insulting Jesus. He says, 'what is wrong with you? We deserve this. Now we are about to die, and you are insulting Jesus? Don't you fear God? Maybe you haven't feared Him your whole life, but now, RIGHT NOW, don't you fear God as your life slips away?'

Well, that shuts up the first guy. He's done talking. The second guy who spoke up, he looks at Jesus and says, 'please remember me when You come into Your kingdom.' Do you understand what he is saying? He knows that they are all dying. For Jesus to be dying on that cross, and for that guy to realize that Jesus is a king, and about to come into His kingdom, it tells me that this second criminal knew who Jesus was. He knew the answer to the most important question. Who is Jesus Christ? This man knows that Jesus is the Messiah, the Savior of the world. He knows that Jesus will rule in the spiritual world. That man is hanging there and can do none of the things to please God that we think are so important. But he has done everything that God thinks is important. He has believed in the name of God's one and only Son, just like it tells us we need to do in John, Chapter Three. He believes, and that's all he needs to do. Jesus answers this man by saying, 'today you will be with Me in Paradise.'"

JD paused again, scanning the crowd before he spoke again.

"What if you die today? Where are YOU gonna be? All you have to do is believe. You can do it right now. Admit that you are a sinner, and that Jesus died for your sins so that you can be forgiven and be with Him in paradise. Don't be stuck out of your Father's house like that older brother who thought he didn't need forgiveness. YOU ARE NOT SO GOOD THAT YOU DON'T NEED GOD'S FORGIVENESS. You are also not so bad that God will not forgive you if you ask for His forgiveness. Just like that younger brother who had screwed up so badly, you have a loving Father who is ready to forgive you and can't wait to welcome you back home. But you have to remember, it's all about who you believe in, not what good things you've been doing. It's all about how you answer that question that Jesus asked His own disciples. WHO IS JESUS CHRIST?

WHAT IS YOUR ANSWER?" JD yelled at the crowd. "WHO DO YOU SAY HE IS? IS HE THE GOD WHO CREATED THE UNIVERSE AND TOOK HUMAN FORM TO COME TO EARTH AND TAKE THE PUNISHMENT FOR YOUR SINS SO THAT YOU CAN BE FORGIVEN AND LIVE IN PEACE WITH HIM FOREVER? WHAT IF YOU DIE TODAY, WHERE ARE YOU GONNA BE? ARE YOU GOING TO BE FORGIVEN AND WELCOMED INTO YOUR FATHER'S HOUSE? WHAT DO YOU BELIEVE? DO YOU BELIEVE IN YOUR OWN GOOD WORKS, OR DO YOU BELIEVE IN THE FORGIVENESS THAT COMES THROUGH FAITH IN JESUS? WHAT IF THAT WAS YOU ON THAT CROSS NEXT TO JESUS? WHAT IF YOU WERE DYING? WOULD JESUS TELL YOU THAT YOU WOULD BE WITH HIM TODAY IN PARADISE? WHERE YOU GONNA BE PEOPLE? WHERE YOU GONNA BE FOREVER?!"

JD was crying as he finished. The crying became sobs that shook his whole body as he repeated the question in a softer voice.

"Where you gonna be? Where you gonna be? Where..."

He was crying so hard that he could no longer speak. Sam picked him up and gently placed him back on the beach. He wrapped his massive arms around his friend and held him as he cried.

"You did good," Sam told his friend. "You did real good brother."

The beach was quiet, except for scattered sounds of crying, and the quiet prayers of new believers.

CHAPTER 27

Lynn was still sitting in the driver's seat of the stolen taxi. Padre had finished changing into his old police uniform as JD finished speaking on the beach. The car was still running as they sat in the parking garage. Lynn had leaned forward against the wheel, holding her head in her hands, crying. Padre reached over, turned the set of keys, and took them out of the ignition. They sat that way for a few minutes in awkward silence.

"What the hell is wrong with you?" Padre finally asked her.

"Haven't you been listening to him?" she asked. "Don't you hear what he is saying about God's love and forgiveness? I've never heard anyone explain it like that. It's all so clear and simple. Don't you see the truth? We're about to die. Don't you care about what comes next?"

"Lynn, I'm not sure what I think about the idea of a loving God who has this master plan worked out because He cares so much for us. I've seen so many good people have their lives torn apart by the bad guys. I've seen them crushed and grieving. I remember when you were a kid and you had those dead eyes from all the crap you went through. How old were you when your mom's boyfriends started touching you? Eleven? Twelve? Do you think that was part of God's loving plan?

Look, I'm open to the idea that there is probably some powerful God who made everything and set it all in motion. But I don't buy that He's still up there controlling everything. There is no way you could have power, say that you love people and are looking out for them, and create the mess that most people live with. Maybe this is hell, and we have to earn our way out.

Look around you, Lynn. You can see the burned-out buildings and smell the dead bodies as we drive by. And we have it good in this country. Most of the rest of the world is a way bigger hellhole than what you see here.

The circular logic is a scam. If things are good, thank God for the blessing. If it's bad, you can't blame God. He has a bigger plan that you just don't understand. I'm not going to spend my life thinking that God will make everything better. I've seen the proof that He doesn't. I'm going to do what I can to make positive changes. If that pisses off God, I'm okay with that. He pisses me off too sometimes."

"Doesn't any of his talk about God forgiving everything you've done wrong because He loves you not make you want that?" Lynn asked. "I can't remember how many people I've killed, or blackmailed, how many lives I've ruined, because it seemed like the right thing to do. I really can't, because I stopped caring, and I've become so numb to everything. I never felt loved by anyone in my life. I used to feel hate. Now I feel nothing. Last night and today, I feel like I've woken up from a bad dream. I feel so ashamed of all the things I've done. I feel like I've woken up and can feel pain and regret again, but I have this peace inside of me that I can't explain. I prayed that prayer with JD. I did it when we were pulling into this garage and he was teaching. I told Jesus that I am a sinner, separated from Him by that sin, but that I know He died for ME, to forgive MY sins, because he loves ME."

She turned to look into Padre's cold blue eyes.

"I can't let you do this," she told him. "I can't let you kill all these people. I'm done with killing, and I won't let you do it. If you try to blow those people up, I'll rat you out to all the soldiers out there on the streets. I don't care if I get in trouble and go to jail too. It's over, Padre. It's over, and I feel so relieved."

Padre hadn't expected this. Lynn had always been on his side. They had always shared the same perspective on how to fight back against their enemies, and how to make the world a better place. Also, she owed him, and they both knew it. HE was the one who had saved her long ago, not some criminal preaching on the radio.

"Are you sure that's how you feel?" he asked her. It wasn't smart, but he wanted to give her a chance to change her mind. "You won't just drive away and let me finish this?"

Lynn looked down and shook her head no.

"Damn it, Lynn!" Padre yelled. "You were the one who insisted on coming with me. You could have stayed behind in Kansas City, but you had to come help. Well, this isn't helping me! I have a duty to try to protect this country. Protecting this country means keeping those people out of power. You KNOW what those leftist assholes will do to this country. They are like locusts; they destroy everything. I will not sit by and let that happen if I can stop it. Do not try to keep me from doing my duty. I need to finish this."

"I won't let it happen," she said quietly.

"You're sure?"

"I'm sure," she said, looking away from him.

Padre struck quickly. Without warning, his left hand moved to cover Lynn's mouth, and his right hand made a fist that gripped the keys so that they stuck out between his second and third knuckles. He swung big, roundhouse swings at Lynn's chest. He could hear the pop of her lungs being punctured as he plunged the keys into her chest. He could hear the crack of broken ribs as the powerful blows crushed both sides of her chest. He continued to hold her mouth closed as she struggled to breathe. Soon the struggling ceased, and she was staring at him without blinking.

"Damn it, Lynn!" Padre said to her corpse as he caught his breath. "Why the hell did you go soft on me? What the hell were you thinking? You know I'm going to finish this mission. This is my duty, and nobody is going to stop me, not even you."

He reached into the back seat for his wheelchair. He locked the wheels and transferred himself into it. He locked the car door and started wheeling himself toward the church. *She would have been dead soon anyway*, the defensive part of his brain said as he wheeled away from the garage. *Keep moving*, he told himself. *The job is almost done.*

CHAPTER 28

Paul and Luke were traveling away from Chicago. They had run through the empty streets and were back at the car before JD started teaching on the beach. Someone had been vandalizing cars in the parking garage where they had parked their car. Several windows were smashed, and several tires had been punctured. Paul breathed a sigh of relief when he saw their car. Someone had spray-painted "BULLS" in bright red letters across the driver's side of the car, but there was no sign of damage that would keep their car from running.

They drove fast through the empty Chicago streets and were soon back on the highway heading south and east. Paul pushed the speed up to 90 on the empty interstate. He decided to speed past all the toll booths as they traveled away from Chicago. He and Luke were quiet, listening to a Chicago radio station covering JD teaching on the beach. As he finished teaching about the two brothers, the local radio talk show host broke in with an announcement.

"We are now going to break away from our live coverage from Lincoln Park. We will get a national news update at the top of the hour after a quick word from our sponsors. When we come back, we will hear from reporters at the downtown Cathedral. People have been arriving early to the Unity rally. We will also get an update from the church where the President will speak later today, and we will check back in with our reporters in Lincoln Park. This is WGN radio. Stay tuned. We will be right back."

Paul turned down the radio as it went to commercial. They were making great time on the empty interstate. They were now heading east toward Iowa.

"What do you think?" he asked Luke as they sped along.

"I wish I had my phone," Luke told his uncle. "It's still back in that trailer we slept in last night. If I had it, I could find a live stream of JD teaching by the Lake. Why did we have to leave?"

"Sam said that we are supposed to go see Grandpa Rich," Paul answered. "He said that God had other plans for us today and it was time for us to leave. I think he was letting me know that we wouldn't get another chance to see Grandpa alive if we didn't get moving."

"That was the most amazing weekend of my life," Luke told his Uncle. "I can't believe what we saw in that park. It feels unreal. Those two guys are awesome. I can't believe that Sam was right about the Homeland Security guy dying this morning."

"I know," Paul responded. "It was amazing watching JD teach. It was great talking to them last night in the trailer. I'm glad we could give JD some encouragement after a long day. I hope they switch back to him soon. I want to hear what else he has to say."

"Me too," Luke said, as they continued to speed away from Chicago.

CHAPTER 29

Hamid was worried. He had come so far, he was so close to accomplishing this great act of martyrdom. He was worried that he would be stopped before he could detonate the bomb in Chicago. He could see the buildings of downtown Chicago. The bomb was armed and the detonator was ready. He simply had to press a button and it would detonate. He knew that the Americans had planes patrolling the skies, scouting for threats. They had electronic surveillance, satellite surveillance, and police patrolling these waters. The plan was to run this boat all the way into one of the marinas near downtown before detonating, if possible. The direct kill radius would be approximately two miles. The fire from the explosion might double that. The fallout from radiation should cover a larger area, but it would depend on so many different weather variables.

Hamid knew that the Americans would try to stop him at some point. If they stopped his boat or killed him too far from land, this would all be a waste. He was checking several windows, moving from one side of the boat to the other, talking to himself as he went.

"No planes, good, very good. No boats near me. One is turning and starting my way. I will need to keep watching that. Over here, nothing to worry about yet. Still no planes."

He continued talking to himself as he moved from window to window in the boat. He had been told not to go up on the deck. He should not be seen. Those were his instructions. He had put Moshen out of his thoughts, thinking that he had killed him with the fire extinguisher.

Moshen had regained consciousness. He was still lying on the floor of the ship's galley. He could hear Hamid talking to himself in the next room. Moshen couldn't remember what had happened to him. He had been at the table listening to the preacher. He remembered Hamid yelling something at him; now he was on the floor, I shouldn't have turned my back on that mean, little man, he scolded himself.

He couldn't seem to take a breath. The pain in his chest was intolerable if he took more than a shallow breath. His left side was not working properly. He was trying to lift his left arm, but nothing was happening. Blood was caked in his right eye. He could see out of his left eye, and he discovered that he could move his right arm and leg. Each movement brought horrible pain, and he became even more short of breath. He used his working right leg to push himself against the kitchen cabinets. It took two tries, but he was able to open the cabinets under the sink. A flare gun. He was hoping for a better weapon, but this would do.

He started to smile at his discovery, but stopped when he realized that his face hurt when he smiled. He didn't know how long he had been unconscious. He was worried that they were close to Chicago and Hamid would detonate the bomb before he could stop him. Using his one working, painful arm, he clumsily grabbed the gun and started for the bedroom. He had to turn his body on the floor and use his right leg to push his body across the floor. The galley was small. He only had to move a few feet to see through the door into the bedroom. Every movement was slow and painful. Every movement seemed to take too long. He needed to stop the bomb from going off. That thought made him push through the pain that had his brain screaming at him to stop moving.

Moshen had moved far enough to see through the door, into the small bedroom. He could see Hamid talking to himself as he moved from window to window. The image of the little scientist and the entire bedroom was becoming blurry. Hamid's voice seemed to be fading, making it sound like Hamid was far away from him. Moshen tried to lift the gun with his 'good' right hand, but now that arm wasn't doing what it was told, just like the left side had earlier.

You have to do this, Moshen told himself as he struggled to stay conscious. Stay awake. It doesn't matter how much you hurt. You must stop him. He was now able to will his right arm to lift the flare gun and point it toward Hamid, but he couldn't keep his hand steady. The small bedroom was no longer blurry; it was all turning black.

Hamid was still focused on the windows and looking for signs of the police ready to stop them. He continued to move from window to window.

"Very good," he muttered to himself. "That plane is circling away. That boat is not coming toward us. Just a little closer, just a little closer."

Hamid quit moving. The window on his left gave him the best view of downtown Chicago as they approached. It was getting harder for Marco to breathe. His vision was fading. He would only get one shot at Hamid. He didn't know if a shot from the flare gun would kill Hamid, but he thought it might incapacitate him enough that he wouldn't be able to detonate the bomb. He tried his best to steady his arm and aim the flare gun.

CHAPTER 30

This made him nervous. Now all he could do was wait. Padre had been able to get into position right in front of the church. He had wheeled himself right up to one of the former President's staff when he arrived at the church. The man he spoke to was setting up the camera shot that would be seen on TV as the former first family walked into the church. This man was directing who would be in the background of that camera shot.

"They told me to come up here and talk to you," Padre told the young man in front of the church. He interrupted two other people who were both trying to talk to the important young stage director. "They told me that I'm supposed to be up front. They said something about having a retired cop in the picture being a good thing."

Padre had left the blanket back at the car, He was sitting tall in the wheelchair, wearing his old police uniform. He had decided to push the retired cop angle, no more hiding under a blanket.

"Who told you that?" the man asked him.

Padre pointed to a group of the former President's staffers clustered in a group down the street. The young man directing the scene in front of the church didn't have time to walk over to the group and argue about who was going to be visible in the background on the shot outside the church. The former President would be here soon, and he didn't have everyone in place. He didn't agree with putting the cop in this shot, but he wasn't in charge. It helped that the cop was in a wheelchair, the man thought to himself, as he decided where to place Padre.

"I want you over there, in the first row behind the roped-off area," the man said, pointing to an area near the church. "The former President and his family will walk in front of you to get into the church. I want you to salute as he walks by."

Then the man was back to dealing with other problems, with other people vying for his attention. Padre took his place behind the roped-off area. When he was questioned about who told him he should be there, he pointed back to the young man he had just lied to. That answer seemed good enough for the people who questioned him.

As he sat in front of the church, waiting for his chance to assassinate the former first family, and all the people on the street around him, he marveled at his good luck. He couldn't believe that this had actually worked out as planned. Well, not everything had gone as planned, he reminded himself, as the memory of killing Lynn flashed in his mind. *It doesn't matter*, he told himself, *we'll all be dead soon*.

He checked his watch. The former President was running late. Padre was nervous. He felt exposed sitting in front of the church. Too many Secret Service agents were at this event looking for potential threats. If he was seen as a threat, this mission would end in failure. *How do I find cover out here in the open*, Padre asked himself. The woman to his right was crying and blowing her nose in a big, white handkerchief. *Bingo*. Padre covered his face with both hands and pretended he was crying. It wasn't much coverage, but it helped ease his mind a little.

One of the women assigned to the Secret Service detail of the former President was across the street from Padre. She was wearing reflective sunglasses that hid her eyes. She had been watching Padre as he wheeled into position outside the church. She turned her head to the left, acting like she was looking down the street, but her gaze stayed on Padre. Something wasn't right about him. He kept covering his face like he was crying, but there were no tears, and his nose wasn't running. As she looked closer, she could see blood on his right hand and on his shirt sleeve. She stepped back into the crowd, and out of Padre's sight. She spoke into her hand, warning the agent across the street about a possible threat.

A few minutes later, the agent she had contacted appeared behind Padre. The man in the dark suit stayed behind Padre, moving from his right to his left. He didn't see any obvious weapons. He reported back to the first agent and let her know that he was moving in for a closer look.

Padre kept his face in his hands, but he could catch glimpses of the Secret Service agent who was watching him. The agent edged closer until he was standing right behind Padre. He was looking for a weapon hidden under the man's clothes, or in his chair. Padre took out his phone, acting like he was going to record the President's walk into the

Church. He dialed the number that would detonate the bomb, but did not yet hit send.

"Am I considered a threat?" Padre asked the Secret Service agent behind him without turning around. The agent was surprised, but quickly regained his composure. He walked up beside Padre.

"My job is to consider everybody a threat. You know that," he told Padre.

Padre laughed at the answer.

"Good point. Are you going to frisk me? You're not some weirdo who wants to do a cavity search, are you?"

The question made the agent smile. A crusty old cop with a sense of humor, I think I like this guy, he thought as the smile disappeared.

"No sir, no cavity search," the agent answered. "We haven't seen a lot of retired cops at this event. What brings you out?"

"I honestly don't know," Padre lied to the agent. "When I was on active duty, I used to think I had all the answers. But I've been watching things fall apart to the point where we have tanks in the street. I was listening to that preacher in Lincoln Park. He keeps talking about forgiveness and second chances. I guess I just wanted to hear what was being said down here today. I guess I'm more open to other answers today than I used to be. I have friends who were killed last weekend. I used to walk these streets with some of those cops. They were good men. I don't even know why they're gone. I guess I want to hear something that makes me think this won't happen again. Maybe the former president can help make sense of this. I sure don't trust the clown that's in the White House now."

Padre didn't know if this agent believed his lies. Those reflective sunglasses made it hard to read him. The important thing was that he was killing time. If he could stall this agent a little longer, the former President and his family would be walking right in front of him.

"I understand," the agent answered. "You know I have to frisk you before we're done. It's not personal, I'm just doing my job."

Padre raised his arms, and the agent performed a quick, but very professional pat-down. As he finished, a cheer went up from the crowd. The former President and his family stepped out of a black suburban and began walking toward the church. He was smiling and waving to the crowd. Padre hated the sight of that man. I'm glad I get to be the one to end his life, Padre thought as he put on a fake smile and clapped with the crowd around him.

The Secret Service agent faded back into the crowd. The only things he had found in Padre's pockets were a set of keys and a wallet. Padre continued to hold the phone while he was frisked, with his thumb ready to hit the send button. As the agent walked away, Padre took his thumb off the send button. He would wait to press send until the target was right in front of him.

The Secret Service agent was talking into his hand, letting the other agents know that Padre did not have a weapon.

"He's not armed," the agent was saying into his hand. "I don't think he's a threat. He said that he used to walk these streets with some of the cops who died Friday. He was crying about that."

The crowd had gotten louder as the former President and his family approached the church. Trailing them was a small herd of party big-shots and future presidential hopefuls. The agent who had frisked Padre was having trouble hearing what was being said in his earpiece because of the crowd noise.

"Please repeat!" he yelled into his hand. "I did not copy that!"

He pressed the earpiece into his ear, trying to hear the response from the agent across the street who had warned about this possible threat.

"Kansas City!" she yelled into her hand. "His uniform says KCPD. He never walked these streets. He lied to you. Get him out of there!"

The agent turned and started pushing his way back through the crowd. One of the agents, on a rooftop overlooking the street, was adjusting the sight on his rifle to target Padre. The former first family was moving slowly, but kept moving closer to the church. Padre could see that the Secret Service agent who had frisked him was pushing his way toward him through the crowd. He was reaching for the gun in his shoulder holster.

Hurry up, Padre thought, watching the politicians moving slowly toward the church. *Keep moving, just a little bit closer*. He needed them close enough to know that the bomb would kill them; being injured wasn't good enough. He needed them dead and gone. His thumb stayed on the send button.

CHAPTER 31

JD had finally stopped crying.

"Was that it?" he asked Sam. "Am I done?"

"Yeah," Sam told him. "You're done. You did great, JD. I'm so proud of you. I remember who you were just a few years ago. It's been amazing watching God change you and use you. I feel so blessed to be a part of that."

"Did you know it was going to be like this?" JD asked him. "Did God show you all of this in your dreams?"

"I saw some, but not all of it," Sam explained. "The dreams skip around in time. I could see that we would finish up here on this beach. I knew you would be discouraged last night. I knew the devil was going to attack you every way that he could, and he came at you hard last night. I'm so glad you didn't give up and you let God keep using you. I've been praying for you day and night for the past two weeks, that's why I was so tired on the drive from Kansas City. I knew you had some battles to go through. You fought through the discouragement and self-doubt, and the desire to just give up and walk away. I'm very proud of you.

I knew that Paul and Luke were coming here to help us. I think God used them to encourage you and redirect you a little bit. I could see that this wasn't going to be where it ended for them. I hope Paul gets a chance to see his dad before he dies. I'm not sure how that will turn out. I hope he has the peace of knowing that his dad became a Christian before he dies, even if he doesn't get to see him. Who knows, maybe his dad was able to watch you teach today. You know you were on TVs all over the country, don't you?"

JD shook his head in amazement.

"I really didn't believe you," JD admitted to his friend. "You told me about preaching to all these people, but I really didn't believe you. All I ever did was preach in jail, to people just like us. It was easy there. I would tell them my story, which was a lot like their own story. I never thought I could reach people like this, out in the real world. Then I was up on your shoulders last night, and all those people were listening, and for a moment, I thought that I was going to preach all night and teach all these people about the God who loves them.

I was up so high, then we got arrested, and it all seemed to be falling apart. All I could think of was that I had failed at the most important thing I was ever supposed to do. I was so low last night, I was ready to give up. Thanks for praying for me. Thanks for always being there."

"You're welcome. It was..." Sam's voice broke. "It was incredible. I feel so lucky to be a part of this."

They were quiet for a moment, as they stared out at the lake, each one lost in his own thoughts.

"It's time for us to go pray on our own," Sam told his friend. "Let them know," Sam said, nodding at the large crowd on the beach.

JD turned away from his friend to address the crowd. He did not get back on Sam's big shoulders.

"I told you all that I'm supposed to tell you," JD told the crowd. "It's time for you to reflect on that message and pray. I think God is at work in a lot of hearts here today. I pray that he opens your hearts to the truth and you are saved. I think that it's time to pray to the God who made you and loves you. I have some things in my heart that I need to talk with God about. I'm sure you do too. It's time to get right with God, people. I want you to picture yourself hanging on that cross next to Jesus. Your time is very short. Open up your heart and talk to the Father who loves you. That's all I've got to say."

With that, he turned and started limping toward Lake Michigan. Walking on the sand was slower and more painful for JD. He limped forty feet from the group, then sat down in the sand to pray, one last time.

Sam hadn't moved. He watched as his friend prayed. *I will miss this*, he thought. He was done carrying JD, done protecting him, done with all the things that had made life so good for the past few years with his friend. There was one more thing for him to do before he finished.

He walked over to Estella, Leroy, and D'Anthony. She had let go of D'Anthony's hand and was quietly crying, with her face in her hands. When Sam put a big hand on her shoulder, she began crying harder. They stood that way until her cries grew quieter.

He leaned in close, so she could hear his soft, raspy voice.

"Don't hold back," Sam told her. "When you're done praying, do what God wants you to do."

He bent down and kissed her on top of her head, then walked back to finish the day with his friend.

JD had finished praying, and for now, had finished crying. He was sitting in the sand, taking off his shoes and socks, and was looking out at the water.

"I have never been to a beach before," he told Sam, as his friend sat down next to him. "This feels good," he said as he pushed his feet into the sand. They sat on the beach quietly, watching the water.

"I never thanked you for saving my life," JD told his friend.

"I think you did," Sam corrected him. "You thanked me more than you will ever know." JD smiled at his friend, then was back to watching the water. "Are you going to take your shoes off?" JD asked his friend.

"Why?" Sam asked, grinning at him. "Do you want one more chance to tell me how bad my feet stink?"

JD laughed out loud. "Was I lying?" he asked Sam. "Everybody knows how bad your feet stink. They were just all too scared to tell you."

Sam reached out and wrapped a big arm around his friend's shoulder.

"I have one last surprise for you this morning," Sam told him. "We get to hear a beautiful song while we sit here on this beach."

"That sounds nice. That sounds like a good way for this to end," JD replied. He paused, then added. "I love you, brother."

"I love you, too, JD."

Then they were done talking. They sat quietly for watching the water. The silence ended as Estella spoke. Her voice carried up and down the quiet beach.

"My heart is full of joy and I need to sing. I need to praise God," Estella told the people gathered on the beach. "This is something I sang in church a long time ago. It's one of my favorites. Y'all can join in if you want."

Her beautiful, rich voice could be heard clearly on the quiet beach as she started in with a song she had learned as a child.

"Amazing grace, how sweet the sound, that saved a wretch like me," voices up and down the beach joined in as she continued. "I once was lost, but now am found, was blind but now I see."

JD began crying again as the singing grew louder on the beach.

CHAPTER 32

Paul and Luke were still speeding on a nearly deserted highway toward Iowa. WGN had shifted their coverage from the beach to coverage of the former President as he approached the church for the self-described 'unity event.' Paul switched from WGN to the local Bott radio affiliate, trying to listen to coverage from the beach. On the car radio, they could hear one of the local Bott radio employees, who was broadcasting from the beach. After hearing JD's talk at the picnic tables Sunday night, the decision had been made to broadcast live from Lincoln Park that morning, hoping to hear JD speak again. The broadcaster from Bott radio had followed JD and Sam down to the beach and was still broadcasting live.

"I've never seen anything like this," he told the radio audience. "I am hearing so many different languages being spoken. These people are on their knees, praying and crying to God. It looks like thousands of people are becoming Christians on this warm Monday in Chicago. This is amazing.

There seems to be a break in the action," he explained to the radio audience. "The two men who have been the focus of activity in Lincoln Park are sitting down on the beach, apart from the rest of the crowd. When we are sure that they are done speaking, we will cut to the speeches at the two events that the current and former President will be attending today. For now, this appears to be where the real story is in Chicago. It is amazing how well this young man can speak publicly and preach from the Bible. According to the press reports I have seen, he didn't finish high school and has had no formal theological training. He appears to be an incredible gifted public speaker who has an excellent grasp of Christianity.

We also continue to receive reports that many non-English speaking people are hearing this man teach in their native tongue. None of that has been confirmed yet. We will keep trying to confirm what we can as we report to you live from Chicago. But now, we will take a commercial break, which we are very late for. I did not want to interrupt this man preaching on the beach this morning, so we will go to a commercial and be back to Chicago very soon."

As the radio went to commercial, Paul and Luke continued to speed away from Chicago. At the same time, Padre was holding his cell phone with his thumb over the send button. The former President and his family were walking closer to his location. Secret Service agents were closing in on him. A boat on Lake Michigan was speeding closer to Chicago. It had gotten the attention of law enforcement, and a Coast Guard boat was moving to intercept the vessel that wasn't responding on the radio.

"Do you want to hear something that's really selfish?" Paul asked Luke. He continued without waiting for Luke to answer, "all I can think about is my dad. I saw all this amazing teaching in Chicago. I guess it was even broadcast all over the country. But all I can think of is that I wish my dad could have been awake and listened to it. He's barely conscious, and will probably die soon. I don't think he's a Christian. If he is, he hides it well. I'm glad we had this amazing weekend in Chicago getting to know those two, and watching JD preach, but I keep thinking about my own dad. I worry he's going to die soon, and that he never believed. I'm worried he's going to spend forever in hell. I feel guilty. I wish I hadn't lost my temper with Rich. I wish I could have stayed right there in Des Moines. Maybe he would have woken up for a little while, and I could have talked to him about becoming a Christian."

"I know you went to Des Moines hoping to reach him," Luke replied. "I'm sorry it didn't work out the way you wanted it to. I was praying for you. Don't give up hope, uncle Paul. Maybe it's not too late."

"Yeah, maybe you're right," Paul answered. He still sounded discouraged. "I guess we'll see in a few hours if little Rich will even let me in his hospital room."

Paul turned the radio back up as the commercials ended, and the voice of Rich Bott could be heard again.

"This is beautiful!" Rich Bott told his audience. "Listen to this."

Estella was singing, with many of the people on the beach joining in. She made it through the first two verses of *Amazing Grace* and was restarting the first verse. She couldn't remember the other verses, and she didn't have the lyrics in front of her. Halfway through the first verse, the singing suddenly stopped. All that could be heard on that channel was static.

Paul turned back to WGN. More static. He hit the seek button to find any station. After several seconds of searching, the channels quit changing. Three ominous beeps could be heard, followed by a recorded voice.

"This is the emergency broadcast system..." the recording began.

This is bad, Paul thought to himself, as he sped away from Chicago. Sam's warning from earlier that morning ran through his mind. *Go west away from the city*, Sam had told him. *When you get to Iowa, get off the main roads. God has other plans for you, my friend. You don't have much time.*

Acknowledgements

I would like to express my deepest gratitude to the remarkable individuals whose teachings have profoundly influenced my understanding of the Bible and shaped the narrative of this book. To John MacArthur, David Jeremiah, Michael Youssef, Alistair Begg, and Tony Evans, your dedication to the Bible and unwavering commitment to sharing the Gospel have been an endless source of inspiration.

Special thanks to Tracy, whose insightful question many years ago ignited a journey of introspection and discovery, ultimately leading to the heart of the message conveyed in these pages.

The author knows that the author is not relevant, but the messsage is.

Printed in the USA
CPSIA information can be obtained
at www.ICGtesting.com
LVHW041930150724
785383LV00004B/5/J

9 781964 296104